POINT BLANK

Fargo had his Henry trained squarely on Drecker's chest, and, at that range, couldn't possibly miss. Drecker tried to clear leather anyway. All Fargo had to do was twitch his trigger finger. But he wanted Drecker alive. So as his enemy drew, Fargo rammed the Henry's barrel into the man's gut, making Drecker double over.

Stern galvanized to life but he was much too late and much too slow. He nearly went cross-eyed when Fargo gouged the rifle's muzzle into his nose.

"Whatever you want, you can have—our horses, our guns, you name it."

The irony of being branded a bandit by a bandit made Fargo grin. "How about the gold ore you stole?" He tossed Stern's revolver in the grass.

"I don't have the slightest idea what you're talking about, mister. I wish to God I did have some gold. I'd be off in New Orleans, living it up." Stern wasn't a good liar.

Fargo smashed the Henry against the man's hip.

Crying out, Stern clutched his side and toppled over. He thrashed wildly about, his face beet red.

"We'll try this again." Fargo shifted so he could slam the rifle against the gunman again if need be. "Keep in mind: I can do this all day." He let that sink in. "Where did you hide the ore?"

THE
TRAILSMAN
#257

COLORADO
CUTTHROATS

by

Jon Sharpe

A SIGNET BOOK

SIGNET
Published by New American Library, a division of
Penguin Putnam Inc., 375 Hudson Street,
New York, New York 10014, U.S.A.
Penguin Books Ltd, 80 Strand,
London WC2R 0RL, England
Penguin Books Australia Ltd, 250 Camberwell Road,
Camberwell, Victoria 3124, Australia
Penguin Books Canada Ltd, 10 Alcorn Avenue,
Toronto, Ontario, Canada M4V 3B2
Penguin Books (N.Z.) Ltd, Cnr Rosedale and Airborne Roads,
Albany, Auckland 1310, New Zealand

Penguin Books Ltd, Registered Offices:
Harmondsworth, Middlesex, England

First published by Signet, an imprint of New American Library,
a division of Penguin Putnam Inc.

First Printing, March 2003
10 9 8 7 6 5 4 3 2 1

The first chapter of this title originally appeared in *High Country Horror,*
the two hundred fifty-sixth volume in this series.

 REGISTERED TRADEMARK—MARCA REGISTRADA

Printed in the United States of America

PUBLISHER'S NOTE
This is a work of fiction. Names, characters, places, and incidents either are the
product of the author's imagination or are used fictitiously, and any resemblance
to actual persons, living or dead, events, or locales is entirely coincidental.

BOOKS ARE AVAILABLE AT QUANTITY DISCOUNTS WHEN USED TO PROMOTE PROD-
UCTS OR SERVICES. FOR INFORMATION PLEASE WRITE TO PREMIUM MARKETING DIVI-
SION, PENGUIN PUTNAM INC., 375 HUDSON STREET, NEW YORK, NEW YORK 10014.

The Trailsman

Beginnings . . . they bend the tree and they mark the man. Skye Fargo was born when he was eighteen. Terror was his midwife, vengeance his first cry. Killing spawned Skye Fargo, ruthless, cold-blooded murder. Out of the acrid smoke of gunpowder still hanging in the air, he rose, cried out a promise never forgotten.

The Trailsman they began to call him all across the West: searcher, scout, hunter, the man who could see where others only looked, his skills for hire but not his soul, the man who lived each day to the fullest, yet trailed each tomorrow. Skye Fargo, the Trailsman, the seeker who could take the wildness of a land and the wanting of a woman and make them his own.

Colorado Territory, 1861—
Murder and deceit run rampant,
and the unwary pay the supreme price.

1

Skye Fargo was having a grand old time. He had three queens and two fours lying facedown on the table in front of him. Behind him was a buxom dove named Molly, skillfully massaging his neck and shoulders. At his elbow stood a half-empty bottle of rotgut. Life didn't get any better. Taking a long swig, he announced, "I raise another twenty." He added the last of his poke to the considerable pot and sat back, as poker-faced as a granite slab.

Two players folded. That left the one they called Garner. Clad in a fine bearskin coat, he was a tall drink of water with a chest as big around as a water barrel. He had been friendly enough during the game, but there was something about him, about his eyes in particular, that hinted he was a troubled man. "I'd never forgive myself if I didn't see this through, hombre," he remarked, and met the raise. "Let's see what you've got."

Fargo savored the moment. His cards had been cold until about half an hour ago when his luck changed. Now there were close to sixty dollars in the pot, the most there had been all evening, and in a few moments it would be his. He flipped his hand over "Read 'em and bawl like a baby."

"Not bad. Not bad at all," Garner said. "Most times a hand like that will do a man proud. But it's not enough." He laid out his own, card by card. "Maybe you'll want to shed a few tears yourself."

Fargo stared. "Four kings beat me all hollow," he admitted, and sighed. There went the last of his money. And any chance he had of renting a hotel room. Tipping the bottle to his mouth, he pushed his chair back. "Count me out, boys. I'm plumb broke." At least he still had his winsome companion. Wrapping his left arm around her slender waist, he started to guide her toward the bar.

"Hold on a second. Did I just hear correctly? You're tapped out?" Molly's button of a nose scrunched up as if she had caught a whiff of dead fish.

"Does it make a difference? We can go to your place after you're done here." Winking, Fargo pecked her on the cheek.

"What about the fancy meal you promised?" Molly's green eyes roved from the dusty crown of his white hat, down over his buckskin shirt and pants, to the tips of his scuffed boots. "I swear! Men are all alike! They have one thing and one thing only on their small minds." Peeved, she ran a hand through her flaming red hair. "After eight hours of work I'll be famished. No meal, no frolic in the hay." She sashayed off.

Fargo let out with another sigh. It wasn't his night. He was beginning to regret ever stopping in Denver. Sure, there were more saloons and doves than just about anywhere west of Kansas City. But it took money to enjoy them. He might as well head for the stable where he had left his Ovaro and sleep in the stall. Letting more coffin varnish sear his throat, he made for the bat-wing doors.

It was hard to believe, but not all that long ago Denver had consisted of a bunch of tents and ramshackle cabins. Now, thanks to the discovery of gold, it was a bustling city whose name had been changed several times along the way. First known as Montana City, it became St. Charles, then Denver City, and now plain Denver.

Easterners were still pouring in, arriving daily by wagon train or stage or on horseback, all eager to make their fortunes. Most were doomed to bitter disappointment. Many would die, victims of the elements or hostiles or human greed. But that didn't stop them from coming.

Fargo breathed deep. Wood smoke laced the cool night air, as did other, less fragrant odors. Turning left, he strolled along a boardwalk fronting a block of stores and saloons, his spurs jingling lightly. Every few steps he treated himself to more whiskey.

Light poured from dozens of windows, bathing a stream of humanity that ebbed to and fro. Townsfolk, gamblers, prospectors, miners, mountain men, and more were all indulging in Denver's infamous nightlife. During the day the city was a model of decorum, with wives and children free to stroll about as they pleased. But after the sun went down Denver underwent a change. The churchgoing segment of the population retired to their homes, and from their lairs emerged the wild and woolly element. Among them were human wolves who prowled the darkened byways in search of easy prey.

Which is why Fargo's lake-blue eyes narrowed when he heard scuffling sounds from the mouth of an alley up ahead, and why his right hand drifted to the smooth grips of his Colt.

Other pedestrians were passing the alley and hardly gave it a second look. An older man, though, paused. He recoiled in horror, made as if to enter, but abruptly changed his mind, shoved his hands into his pockets, and kept on walking. As he passed by Fargo, he averted his face as if ashamed of himself.

The sounds grew louder. Fargo heard the distinct thud of blows mixed with sadistic cackles. He reached the alley and stopped to take another sip.

Four men ringed a skinny figure on the ground. They were a big, burly bunch who at first glance could be mistaken for miners. But their tied-down holsters marked them as men who made their living with their guns, not with picks and shovels. They were taking turns kicking their victim and laughing when he grunted in pain.

It was none of Fargo's business and he started to move on. But then the figure on the ground raised a pale face and cried out, "Please, mister! Enough! I'm sorry!"

"I bet you are, brat!" responded one of the four, his brawny fists clenched. "I'll teach you to try to steal my money!"

"But I wasn't!" the boy cried. "All I did was bump into you!"

Fargo scowled. He could tell the kid was lying. Footpads and pickpockets were as thick as fleas on an old coon dog, and widely despised. The boy had brought the beating on himself for being so stupid.

"Sure you did!" the brawny man growled. "That's why your fingers were in my back pocket!" The man delivered a kick that doubled the boy in half. "You lying sack of puke. Bull Mulligan wasn't born yesterday!" He kicked the boy again, down low.

One of the others chortled. "Pound him into the dirt, Bull! Break every damn bone in his body!"

"That's exactly what I'm fixing to do, Pierce." Mulligan raised his right boot to stomp on the stripling's face.

Fargo couldn't say what made him do what he did next. Entering the alley, he said quietly, "I reckon that's enough. The boy has learned his lesson."

Bull Mulligan glanced around. Disbelief twisted his swarthy features. "Who the hell asked you to butt in?"

Pierce was glaring. "If you know what's good for you, stranger, you'll mind your own damn business."

The boy looked at Fargo. He was in agony, his teeth clenched, trying hard not to cry out. He didn't plead for help. He just looked.

Mulligan brought his boot crashing down. At the last instant the boy jerked his head aside but the heel caught him a glancing blow on the cheek, enough to daze him and start blood trickling from his nose. Bull Mulligan raised his leg to do it again.

"I said that's enough," Fargo warned.

Pierce and the others turned. "What's this kid to you,

4

mister? Are the two of you in cahoots?" Pierce demanded.

"I've never seen him before." Fargo took another sip. He was mildly annoyed at himself for putting his life at risk for a petty thief. The gunmen were taking his measure, and the alley might erupt in gunfire at any moment.

Bull Mulligan shouldered past his friends and halted with his hands on his hips, his right hand inches from a British-made Cooper pistol. "You don't look like a Bible-thumper. And you're sure as hell not a meddling do-good townsman. So give me one good reason why I should stop, or get the hell out."

"Pick any reason you like. But you're done beating him."

"Is that a fact?" Bull Mulligan grinned at his companions, then stabbed for the Cooper.

Fargo had his Colt out and up before the other man cleared leather. He slammed the barrel against Mulligan's temple. For most that would be enough to flatten them. Bull Mulligan, though, was aptly named. The blow rocked him on his heels, but that was all. Fargo struck him a second time, then a third, and sprang back, covering the others as Mulligan oozed to the dirt like so much tree sap. "Anyone else?"

Pierce had started to claw at his six-gun, a Manhattan Navy, as they were called, but now he froze, stupefied by the outcome, his fingers hooked above his revolver.

"Raise your hands! All of you!"

They hesitated. A crafty expression came over Pierce's face, and he growled, "You might get one or two of us, but not all three. If we go for our guns you're as good as dead."

Fargo hoped to avoid gunplay. He would rather bluff them into backing down. But from the way they stood there with their bodies as rigid as boards, their elbows partially crooked to draw, it wasn't working. Then a strange thing happened. Their gazes drifted past him and a look of unease replaced their fury.

5

"What's going on here?"

The voice was familiar. Pivoting so his back was to a building, Fargo warily regarded the newcomer.

It was Garner. He had shoved his bearskin coat aside to reveal a nickel-plated, ivory-handled Remington, and he stood in the alley mouth, glowering at the hard cases who ringed the boy. "I'm waiting for an answer," he prompted.

"These four were kicking the kid into the ground," Fargo said, nodding at the youth. The boy had risen onto an elbow and gingerly pressed a palm to a split cheek.

"Why?" Garner demanded, staring hard at Pierce.

"It was Bull's doing!" Pierce bleated. "The kid tried to pick his pocket so we hauled the runt in here and were teaching him the error of his ways when this bastard stuck his nose in. He pistol-whipped poor Bull."

Garner stalked past Fargo and poked Mulligan with a boot. "I'm impressed. There aren't many hombres who could do this," he said thoughtfully, and then raised his head to glower at Pierce and the others. "I can't leave you idiots alone for more than five seconds, can I?"

"You know them?" Fargo asked, but he was ignored.

Garner suddenly advanced and grabbed Pierce by the front of his shirt. Shaking the smaller man as a grizzly might shake a marmot, Garner grated, "What did I tell you before I went to the saloon? What were my exact words?"

"Not to get into a ruckus or do anything to draw attention." Pierce was scared and it showed.

"Don't draw any attention," Garner repeated. In an amazing display of physical strength, he lifted the other man clear off the ground so that they were nose to nose. "Tell me. What part of that didn't you understand?"

"Why are you taking this out on me?" Pierce squawked. "Bull's to blame! And he was provoked, I tell you!"

"Is that a fact?" Garner shoved Pierce against the

other two gunmen with such force that all three nearly spilled to the dirt. "If you jackasses can't follow orders, maybe you'll be replaced with others who can." He wheeled toward the street. "Pick up that gob of spit and drag him with us. I'll tend to his worthless hide later." Pausing, he glanced at Fargo. "As for you, buckskin, I'd have the done the same thing if I found them first. You're off the hook this time."

Fargo stepped to the boardwalk and watched them file around a corner. He twirled the Colt into its holster and was about to move on when the boy called out.

"Hold on there, mister! I want to thank you for helping me."

The boy was on his knees, an arm across his gut, fumbling with a cap that had fallen off in the scuffle. Grimacing, he pushed to his feet and shuffled over. Blood trickled from several cuts besides the gash on his cheek and he had a knot on his forehead the size of a hen's egg. Gamely, he offered a grimy hand. "I'm Billy Arnold. I'm extremely pleased to make your acquaintance."

"I can't say the same," Fargo bluntly responded without shaking. "You nearly got me shot." He took a few steps but the boy gripped his sleeve.

"I didn't catch your name."

"That's because I didn't give it." Fargo continued on but in a few strides acquired a shadow at his right elbow.

"Any chance you can spare a dollar?" Billy Arnold asked. "I'm sorry to pester you like this, but honest to God I haven't eaten in pretty near two days." As if it were trained to act up on cue, his stomach rumbled.

The kid had a lot of gall, Fargo reflected. "You can starve to death for all I care," he responded. "Maybe if you found a job instead of picking pockets for a living, you could afford to buy food." The boy started to speak but Fargo held up a hand, silencing him, and left him standing there with his mouth hanging open.

The mention of food set Fargo's own stomach to

growling and he tried to silence it with whiskey. It didn't work. To make matters worse, he felt a rare headache coming on. The sooner he turned in, the better.

The stable was on a side street. Not far from it a young couple were locked in a heated embrace and paid no attention as Fargo ambled by. He was almost to the stable doors when he heard the soft patter of someone rushing up behind him, and thinking he was being attacked, he spun and drew.

"My word! Is this the thanks I get for chasing you down?" Molly had a shawl around her shoulders and was toting a handbag. Enticing perfume wreathed her like a fragrant cloud. Sniffing in irritation, she smoothed her shawl. "I thought you had better manners than most of the lunkheads I put up with."

"How was I supposed to know who it was?" Fargo returned the Colt to its holster. "What are you doing here, anyhow? If that bartender claims I didn't pay for the bottle, he's loco."

"I came to apologize for being rude."

Things were finally going Fargo's way. Of all the doves at the Aces High, Molly had attracted him the most. With her lustrous red hair, an hourglass body most women would die for, and a sultry face as smooth and unblemished as expensive china, she was the kind of woman a man would give his eyeteeth to spend ten minutes with. "I thought you had your heart set on a fancy meal."

"I did. But that's no excuse for how I treated you." Molly fussed with her hair. "You were nice to me. You bought me all the drinks I wanted. And you weren't pawing me every second like most men do. So how about we go to your place and make ourselves comfortable?"

"My horse might not care for the company."

"Your horse?" Molly blinked, glanced at the stable, and laughed. "Oh. I get it. You really are flat broke, aren't you?" Grinning, she hugged him close, her more than ample bosom cushioned against his chest. "Fair enough. What say we go to my place instead? It's not much. But the bed is comfy and I might be able to rustle us up a bowl of leftover stew."

Fargo's stomach rumbled again, loud enough to be heard in Missouri.

"I'll take that as a 'yes,' " Molly joked, entwining her arm with his. "Permit me to lead the way."

East of the saloon district, frame homes had sprouted like tidy rows of corn, some framed by white picket fences and boasting flower beds or tiny gardens. Molly rented a pair of second-floor rooms in a house owned by a store clerk who turned in every evening punctually at seven.

"We have to be mighty quiet," she whispered. "My landlord's not a prude but he won't take kindly to my having a male visitor at this hour." Rummaging in her bag for a key, she dug it out and inserted it into the lock.

Fargo went to follow her in, but stopped. A feeling came over him, the feeling of being watched, a sensation he often experienced in the wild and one which he had learned to ignore at his peril. He peered intently from under his hat brim into the surrounding darkness for a sign of whoever was there. He saw no one. He entered the apartment just as Molly lit a lamp and a rosy glow washed over a comfortably furnished room.

Fargo was closing the door when he heard her gasp and exclaim, "What the hell are you doing here?" Whirling, he spied a man seated in a rocking chair in a far corner. The intruder wore an expensive brown suit, an immaculate bowler, and polished shoes. The silver chain of a pocket watch dangled from his vest. He was a man of means and, from the cold stare he bestowed on Fargo, quite unhappy to find Molly wasn't alone.

"Dirkson! How in blazes did you get in here?"

"Your landlord has a spare key, my dear," the man suavely responded. "And he was quite agreeable to admitting me once I'd greased his palm with twenty dollars. After all, he's seen the two of us together often enough. He knows how much I mean to you."

Molly tossed her handbag onto a table and marched over to the rocking chair. Hands on her hips, she snapped, "When are you going to get it through that thick skull of yours that it's over? I don't want to see you anymore. Not now. Not ever again. I want you completely out of my life."

"You don't mean that. You can't." Dirkson nodded at Fargo. "Send this bumpkin away so we can talk in private."

Her jaw clenched, Molly pointed at the door. "Get out of here, Dirkson!"

"Call me Matt, as you've always done. Using my last name is so formal, and after all we've done together, hardly fitting." With his mouth curled in an oily smile, Dirkson reached for her but she recoiled.

Fargo had listened to enough. "You heard the lady, mister. You're leaving whether you want to or not."

Dirkson made a teepee of his fingers. "I wouldn't get involved, were I you. This is a personal matter between the two of us."

"There is no *us*!" Molly practically shouted. "It's been over for weeks now but you can't get that through your thick skull."

"Now, now, my dear." Dirkson's condescending tone was an insult in itself. "You're a woman, and everyone knows how fickle women are. They never know their own hearts."

Shaking her head in exasperation, Molly backed to the table. "He and I kept company for a year or so," she said to Fargo. "I thought he was courting me with an eye to marriage. But then I found out I wasn't the only girl he was seeing. There were two or three others. And he wanted the same thing from all of us."

"Honestly, my dear," Matt Dirkson said stiffly. "Did you really think I would jeopardize my standing in the community by marrying a woman who—" He caught himself, but it was too late.

"A woman who what?" Molly bristled. "Who works in a saloon? Who is a bit too friendly with some of the men she meets? A woman like me?" Storming to the door, she flung it wide. "Get the hell out of here before I throw you out."

"You're hardly capable of evicting me."

"Maybe she's not, but I am." Fargo's temper was getting the better of him. He started toward the rocking chair but Dirkson jumped to his feet and elevated his hands, palms out.

"All right. All right. I can take a hint. If she wants me to go, I'll go. But this isn't the end of it, not by a long shot."

"Yes, it is." Gripping Dirkson by the arm, Fargo hauled him across the room. "Leave. And don't ever come back."

"I don't like being manhandled," Matt Dirkson protested. Without warning, his free hand disappeared under his jacket and reappeared holding a derringer. He leveled it.

Fargo twisted aside at the instant the derringer went off. The *crack* was loud in the confines of the room, as was the thud of the slug hitting the wall. Grabbing Dirkson's wrist, Fargo slammed his knee into the man's elbow. Dirkson screeched and tried to jerk loose but Fargo held on, balled his other fist, and smashed the rejected suitor full in the mouth.

His arms flailing, Dirkson staggered against the table. It saved him from falling, but the derringer fell from his hand. He swiftly bent to retrieve it.

Fargo wasn't about to let him. Taking two quick steps, he kicked Matt Dirkson in the side of the head. Dirkson struck the floor with a resounding crash, made a feeble effort to rise, but collapsed, unconscious.

"Damn him!" Molly exclaimed. "My landlord isn't going to like this!"

Sure enough, within thirty seconds heavy steps heralded a loud pounding on the door. "Miss Williams! Miss Williams! What was all that horrible racket? Open up this instant!"

The landlord had hastily thrown a robe over his nightshirt but neither were ample to cover his rotund bulk. To Fargo, he resembled nothing so much as a human wagon wheel, only larger. "I distinctly heard a gunshot!" His thick lips quivering, he barreled inside and stopped short at the sight of the figure sprawled on the floor. "As I live and breathe, what have you done to Mr. Dirkson? Is he dead?"

"No, but I wish he was!" Molly was a she-cat coiled to pounce. "You had no right letting him in without my permission."

Indignant, the landlord pulled his robe together. "Don't try to shift the blame for this incident to me, young lady! I thought I was doing you a favor. If you'll recall, the last I knew, there was talk of matrimony between Mr. Dirkson and you." He saw Fargo. "And who in the world is this, might I ask? What part has he played in this affair?"

"It's none of your business."

"I beg to differ," the landlord rejoined. "I won't have strangers in my house at all hours. I'm afraid you leave me no recourse but to insist you vacate the premises by this time tomorrow or I'll have you evicted."

"Just hold your horses!" Molly declared. "You know how hard it is to find good accommodations."

"That's your problem," the landlord huffed. "Now, if you'll excuse me—"

Fargo beat him to the doorway and casually placed a hand on his Colt. "You're not being fair. The lady's right. It isn't her fault. She doesn't deserve to be evicted."

"And what will you do if I make her go anyway?"

No words were necessary. Fargo simply locked eyes with the human bowl of pudding.

The landlord blanched. Defiance gave way to budding

uncertainty, which in turn gave way to blatant fear. His Adam's apple bobbed a few times, and he nervously coughed. "Very well. Never let it be said I'm unreasonable. But I insist Mr. Dirkson and you leave or I'll notify the marshal." Having recovered some of his dignity, the landlord straightened to his full, less-than-considerable height. "Agreed?"

Fargo glanced at Molly. Her disappointment was as keen as his but they had no choice and they both knew it. So much for some stew and a fun frolic under the sheets. "Agreed."

Some days nothing went right.

2

It took a few seconds for Fargo to realize where he was. First he smelled the straw his face was buried in, then he heard a nicker and a thump. He opened his eyes and promptly regretted it when his head throbbed with pulsing waves of pain. Sluggishly rising onto his elbows, he bumped the empty whiskey bottle by his side and sent it skittering across the stall.

A shadow moved across him, and the Ovaro's muzzle nuzzled his neck.

"Morning, big fella," Fargo said with lips that felt wooden. Bracing a hand against the stall, he slowly rose. The throbbing grew worse. Normally, it took a lot more than one measly bottle to give him a hangover. This was what he got for swilling the cheap stuff, and from an unlabeled bottle, no less. For all he knew, the bartender brewed it in an old tub out back of the saloon.

Low laughter fell on his ears. Fargo swivelled his protesting eyes toward an aged bean pole sweeping out the aisle. "Something strike your funny bone, old-timer?"

"Sonny, if I looked as green at the gills as you do, I'd shoot myself and put me out of my misery."

Fargo's mouth felt like it was filled with wool. He swallowed a few times, then shuffled stiffly from the stall and on out of the stable. The sun hung midway to noon; he had slept half the morning away. Removing his hat, he shambled over to a horse trough, took a breath, and plunged his head into the water. The shock to his senses jarred him fully awake. Uncoiling, he shook himself like a rain-drenched wolf and sent drops of water flying every which way.

"Mister, you sure look pitiful."

Fargo crooked his head to the left. A street urchin was watching him in undisguised glee. A boy who couldn't be more than fifteen, his clothes streaked with grime and torn in five or six places. A youth with a gashed cheek and a knot the size of a hen's egg on his brow. "Shouldn't you be picking pockets somewhere?"

Billy Arnold's grin evaporated. "You're as hard as iron inside, mister. You know that?"

Fargo sat on the edge of the trough and tilted his head back to let the sun warm his face. "Go annoy someone else, kid. I don't hold thieves in high account."

"But that's just it."

"Just what?" Fargo jammed his hat back on. His day was starting out as the last one had ended—badly. It was high time he bid Denver so long and lit a shuck for parts unknown.

"It's why I followed you last night. I want to talk to you about an idea I had."

Fargo remembered the sensation of being spied on at Molly's. He'd felt it again when he left her place, on his way to the stable. "So that was you." He had to hand it to the kid. Not once had he caught sight of him.

"You knew I was following you the whole time?" Billy asked in undisguised amazement.

"I spend most of my time in the wilds where a man has to have senses as sharp as an animal's." Fargo let it go at that.

"That's exactly what I want to talk about." Billy edged closer as if unsure of what would happen. "All I ask is five minutes of your time to hear me out."

Up close, Fargo could see that the youth's clothes

15

clung to his thin frame like sheets on a clothesline. The kid was skin and bones. "Five minutes. Then run on home to your parents."

With bitter vehemence Billy declared, "I don't have any parents and I sure as hell don't have a home! I live off the street, mister, using my wits to get by the best I can."

"They weren't much help last night, were they?" Again Fargo struck a nerve but it gave him no satisfaction. Placing his hands on the trough, he noted the boy's hopeful expression. "Speak your piece."

Billy perched on the other end of the trough. "Before I say what's on my mind, I have a confession to make. You were right about me. I did try to pick that jasper's pockets. If you hadn't come along when you did, they'd have busted me up for sure."

Fargo patiently waited for him to get to the point.

"I know stealing is wrong. I only do it when I can't rustle up enough money for a meal some other way. And that includes trying to land a job. They aren't easy to come by at my age. Hell, even when I do get one, I'm paid pennies." Billy became downcast. "The other day I spent three hours helping to clean a store and the son of a bitch storekeeper paid me only fifteen cents. The money-grubbing bastard!"

"Quit your cussing," Fargo found himself saying, much to his considerable surprise. "You're too damn young to talk like that." Rather gruffly, he asked, "What does all this have to do with me?"

Billy blinked, then responded, "I'm from New York City. My mother died when I was four. She got sick one day and wasted away. My father turned to drink. Five years later it killed him. The state wanted to put me in a home for boys but I couldn't stand the notion of being penned in with a hundred other kids, so I ran off and took to doing what I've done ever since—"

"Didn't you have any relatives who would look after you?" Fargo interrupted.

"Just an uncle who had seven kids of his own and didn't want another mouth to feed." Billy's shoulders sagged and he bit his lower lip. "I can't blame him, I guess. But it sure was rough those first few years. If I told you some of the scrapes I was in, it'd turn your hair white."

Fargo suppressed a grin. "How did you get from New York City to the Rockies?"

"I scraped up enough money for stage fare to Saint Louis, then hid in a freight wagon bound for Denver. Halfway across the prairie one of the mule skinners found me and took his whip to my back. But they brought me the rest of the way." Billy reached behind him, rubbed his shoulder, and winced at the memory. "Ever since I've been barely scraping by. A few pennies here, a few pennies there. The most I ever had at any one time was two dollars and I spent that on shoes."

"You still haven't said where I fit in."

Billy looked at him. "Teach me how to be like you."

To stall, Fargo squinted up at the sun. Now he understood what all this had been leading up to. But the kid was asking the impossible. "Look at me, boy. Some people would call me a rake and a scoundrel. I drink. I gamble. I like women. And I'm always looking to see what's over the next horizon." He shook his head. "Find someone better to imitate."

"I don't care about stuff like that. It's what you are that counts." Billy paused. "You're a frontiersman. You know how to live off the land, how to hunt and track and find your way in the mountains. How to be beholden to no one but yourself."

"But I've never taken anyone under my wing before—" Fargo began.

"So? You were young once, weren't you? And I bet someone taught you how to do all the things you do, just as I'd like you to teach me." Billy stood up. "*Please*, mister. A couple of weeks of your time is all I'm asking."

There was no denying the youth was sincere. "Why

17

me, boy?" Fargo quizzed him. "Out of all the scouts, mountain men, and whatnot who pass through Denver every month, why pick me?"

"Because you helped me, mister, when few others would. You risked your own life to save mine. That says a lot about the kind of man you must be." Billy stepped closer. "So how about it? I know I'm asking a lot but I'm tired of living hand-to-mouth. Of going days without food." His voice dropped to a whisper. "I don't like having to steal just to fill my belly."

Fargo lowered his chin to his chest. As much as he would like to help, it took years to learn how to live off the land. Even then, staying alive was a challenge. "I'm sorry, boy. I truly am. You'll have to find someone else."

Billy sat back down, his body slumped in despair. "I thought for sure you were the one," he said, more to himself than to Fargo. "I thought for sure you were different from the rest. I guess you've never been all by your lonesome with no one else to turn to."

The statement knifed through Fargo like a sword. All too vividly, memories of his own troubled past rose unbidden in his mind. Memories he usually kept locked away in a vault deep inside of him where they wouldn't be disturbed. How long ago had it been?

Fargo knew all too well what it was like to be alone. Those first years after his parents died had been the roughest of his life. If not for a few helping hands here and there, he might not have made it. "Hell," he said, and rose.

Billy Arnold wouldn't look at him. "Sorry I bothered you, mister. You don't have to worry none about me pestering you anymore."

"I can give you a week. It's nowhere near enough, but you'll be able to make do without picking pockets."

The boy leaped erect, his budding joy a wonder to behold. "You mean it? No joshing?"

"No joshing." Fargo held out his hand and introduced himself. "I don't know about you but I'm starved, so we'd better see about rustling up something to eat." A hitch occurred to him. "I don't suppose you have a horse or a gun tucked away somewhere?"

"No, sir. All I have are the clothes on my back and this." Billy slid a small folding knife from a pocket and pried at the short blade. It was pitted with rust and the tip had been snapped off, but he proudly held it up. "A fella gave me this once out of the goodness of his heart."

"Double hell." Fargo walked into the stable. The old man was still sweeping. "Any chance you would let me have a horse for a couple of hours free of charge?"

The old man stopped in midsweep. "You must be half-drunk yet. Or else you think I'm loco."

Fargo indicated Billy, who stood in the doorway grinning like a simpleton. "I want to take him up into the hills and teach him how to hunt."

"I take that back. You're the one who's loco."

Billy skipped forward as eagerly as a puppy anxious for a bone. "Please, mister. He's telling the truth. We won't be gone long and we'll bring your horse back. My word of honor."

"Sonny, even if I wanted to, it would cost me my job if I let you have a cayuse without paying. The owner isn't big on charity." The old man leaned his broom against a stall.

"How about if I let you hold onto my bedroll and saddlebags?" Fargo proposed.

"Are they crammed full of gold?"

"If they were I'd *buy* a damn horse."

"Then keeping them doesn't do me much good if you don't show up, does it?" The liveryman scratched his grizzled chin. "Although, now that I think of it, we might be able to work something out after all."

Fifteen minutes later Fargo and Billy Arnold rode westward out of Denver along a winding dirt road.

Billy sat tall in the sorry excuse for a saddle the old man had lent them, grinning from ear to ear. "I can't believe he let us have this horse for nothing."

Fargo could. It was about four weeks shy of being turned into glue, so old and decrepit it was a wonder it was breathing.

"I like how its back dips in the middle," Billy remarked. "Makes riding it as comfortable as sitting in an easy chair."

Rolling his eyes skyward, Fargo started to flick his reins to bring the Ovaro to a trot, but then thought better of the idea. Any pace faster than a brisk walk might kill the swayback. "All right. Let's start your lessons. How good are you at telling distance?"

Billy shrugged. "I've never had to try."

Fargo pointed at the distant snow-capped crown of Long's Peak. At over fourteen thousand feet, it was one of the highest along the front range. "How far northwest of us would you say that mountain is?"

"That's northwest? How can you tell without a compass?"

"You have to learn to use your own sense of direction to guide you. At night the stars help, and during the day you go by the sun."

Craning his head back, Billy asked, "How does that work exactly?"

"It's easy." Fargo was baffled by the confused glance the boy gave him until the obvious explanation dawned. "Tell me. Which direction does the sun rise in the morning?"

"Someone told me once but I forget. I think it's south."

Fargo reminded himself the youngster was city bred, and when it came to the basics of woodlore, most city dwellers were as ignorant as rocks. Drawing rein, he dismounted. "Climb down." After Billy obeyed, he went on. "Where's the sun right now?"

"Right there." Billy bobbed his head. "Look up. You can't miss it."

Mentally counting to ten, Fargo clarified what he

meant. "What part of the sky is it in? East, west, north, or south?"

"How should I know?" Confused, Billy gnawed on his lower lip.

"The sun rises in the east and sets in the west." Fargo swept his arm in an imaginary arc. "So in the morning it's in the eastern half of the sky, in the afternoon it's in the western half. At noon it's overhead."

"But it's not noon yet," Billy threw in. "I saw the clock on the bank on the way out of Denver. It can't be later than eleven." His forehead furrowed a few moments, then he exclaimed, "I've got it! If it's still morning, that means the sun is in the eastern half of the sky!"

"Good. Now stand sideways to the sun with your arms out from your sides, your right arm pointing to the east and your left arm toward where the sun will set."

Billy had to shift around a few times before he got it right. "Like this?"

"Just like that. If you do it correctly, your right arm will always be east, your left arm will point west, you'll be facing north, and your hind end will be to the south."

"That's all there is to it?" Billy laughed with glee. "Heck, being a frontiersman is easier than I thought."

"What if it's cloudy? Or foggy? Or raining or snowing? What if you're in a forest? Or a valley where high peaks blot out the sun?" Fargo rattled off the list to puncture the boy's premature bubble of confidence. "There's a lot more to telling where you are. Don't get cocky."

They remounted and pushed on toward the emerald foothills. Darkling buzzards circled to the south, while to the west a golden eagle soared on outstretched wings. At one point a startled rabbit bounded from their path. At another, several does burst from a thicket and raced off into the brush.

Billy acted like a five-year-old who had never been out of doors. He was interested in everything, and badgered Fargo with a hundred and one questions about the wildlife and the plant life. Each answer sparked a new question. Secretly, Fargo was pleased by the boy's unquenchable thirst for knowledge. The more Billy was willing to learn, the better he would become.

"Every creature has its habits," Fargo said in answer to the umpteenth query. "Know what those habits are and you'll never go hungry."

"Such as?"

"Deer like to hole up during the day. They're most active at night when it's harder for the meat eaters to catch them. Whitetails will flash the whites of their tails when they run off. Mule deer, which are found at higher elevations, have a stiff-legged gait that's hard to describe. The best time to hunt both is at dawn and dusk."

"What about bears? What do you suggest if I run into one?"

"If it's a black bear, nine times out of ten it'll skedaddle the other way. The tenth time you can usually bluff it into leaving you alone. But there's no predicting grizzlies at all. Sometimes they'll run, sometimes they'll come after you. Whatever you do, never go near a bear with cubs." Fargo shucked his Henry rifle from its saddle scabbard. "When you make camp at night, don't leave food lying around. It'll draw in every bear for miles around."

Billy was soaking up the information like a sponge soaked up water. "I heard those mule skinners say they're more scared of rattlesnakes than they are of bears. Why would that be?"

"Rattlers can spook horses and mules into running off and stampede cattle to hell and back. Keep your eyes skinned when you're in rocky country. Snakes love to sun themselves during the hottest part of the day, and sometimes they blend right into the rocks they're lying on." A hint of movement high on a hill drew Fargo's interest. "Rattlers are also dangerous at night. That's when they do most of their hunting, which is why you always keep your boots on until you're ready to turn in.

22

And if one crawls into your blankets, whatever you do, don't make any sudden moves."

"They don't do that!" Billy laughed. "You're trying to scare me."

"Snakes like to keep warm, boy. To them, your body is a fireplace on a cold night. A scout I know once had a big snake crawl in with him early one night and he lay there until noon the next day without twitching a muscle."

"Then what? It bit him?"

"He took a chance and peeked under his blanket. It was a garter snake. He was so mad, he killed it, skinned it, and ate it for supper."

Billy shuddered. "You'll never catch me eating a snake."

"To a starving man all meat looks the same. If you're hungry enough you'll eat anything." Fargo detected a game trail leading toward the crest of an adjacent hill and kneed the stallion up it. "Which reminds me. If friendly Indians ever invite you for a meal, eat whatever is put in front of you or they'll take it as an insult."

"What kinds of things do they eat?"

"The Cheyenne like roast dog. Shoshones are fond of raw deer intestines. Up north you might be offered moose eyes."

Billy contorted his face as if he had sucked on a lemon. "Thanks, but no thanks. If they invite me to supper I'll just say I'm feeling poorly and bow out."

"It wouldn't sit well. A man on his own in the wild can't afford to get on their bad side. Win an Indian's friendship and he'll give you the shirt off his back. Rile him and he'll never forget it."

Thick scrub spread before them. Fargo focused on the spot where he had registered movement and was rewarded with a distinct silhouette. Reining up, he waited for the swayback to come up alongside him, then thrust his rifle at the kid. "Ever fired one of these before?"

"Can't say as I have. My father didn't own a gun. And

I sure haven't been able to afford one." Billy was admiring the golden brass receiver. "It sure is shiny. Is it a Spencer?"

"A Henry, .44-caliber rimfire. It uses metal cartridges. Holds fifteen in the magazine." With it, Fargo could bang off thirty shots in under a minute, a superior rate of fire to any firearm on the market. "I'll let you take first crack at the buck above us. You need to learn how to shoot and now is as good a time as any."

Billy held the rifle against his side, his thumb on the hammer. "What buck? All I see are a few sparrows."

"Look to the right of them, low in the thicket. See the thing that looks like a leaf moving in the wind? It's one of the buck's ears."

"You're imagining things." Billy peered intently at the spot for all of half a minute, then declared, "I'll be switched! I see it now! The head and antlers and everything! It's lying on the ground with just its head showing. That's pretty clever."

"Deer don't live to a ripe old age by standing out in the open wearing a sign that says *Shoot Me*." Fargo pointed. "Aim between the right eye and the ear."

Billy tried to sight down the barrel but he was holding the rifle too low.

"Here." Fargo moved the Henry so the stock was tight against the boy's shoulder. "Place your cheek like so, then line up the front and rear sights. The bead at the end of the barrel should be right where you want the slug to hit. There's already a round in the chamber, so all you have to do is pull back the hammer and squeeze the trigger when you're ready."

Again Billy took aim. This time he did so properly. The click of the hammer was loud in the stillness. He slid his forefinger around the trigger and was all set.

Fargo braced for the blast but the seconds crawled by and it never came. "Is something the matter?"

"There's something you should know. I've never killed anything before."

"Never?" Fargo began to think the boy was out of his

24

element in more ways than one. Some people didn't have the grit it took to confront nature on its own terms. They were too kindly for their own good.

"I shot a bird with a slingshot for fun when I was six. Crippled it. My father took a switch to me and promised if I ever did something like that again, he'd use a cane next time."

"This is different. You're not killing the buck for fun. You're killing it to eat, to keep yourself alive. It's him or you. Make up your mind." When Billy still didn't shoot, Fargo said, "Maybe we should go back. You're greener than grass, and I doubt you'll change any time soon. We'll try to land you a job at a store. Or maybe the old buzzard at the stable can use help sweeping out the horseshit."

The boom of the Henry rolled off across the hills and echoed among the towering peaks beyond. At the shot, the buck sprang from the thicket and raced up the slope, seemingly unaffected. But it traveled only fifty or sixty feet before its front legs buckled and it pitched forward and did a complete somersault, ending up on its back with its legs thrashing wildly. But only for a few moments. With a convulsive heave, it rolled onto its side and was still.

"That was a fine shot."

Stunned by his feat, Billy was a statue. Then a broad smile lit his face and he pumped the Henry in the air. "I did it!" he yipped in pure joy. "Did you see? All by myself!"

Grinning, Fargo skirted the thicket. A trail of brightly glistening scarlet drops led to the buck. Swinging off of the pinto, Fargo opened a saddlebag and took out a new skinning knife he had recently bought. Manufactured by the Green River Knife Company, it had a curved blade to make it easier to slice through thick tendons and muscle, a full-length tang, and a dark brown finish on the handle. "Climb on down, boy. You killed it, you get to skin it."

25

Billy was staring aghast at the wide exit hole the slug had made. "Can't you do the honors?" he squeamishly asked.

"You have to learn sometime."

Reluctantly, Billy slid to the ground. "I don't know if I'm up to this." He gazed past Fargo, back the way they came. "Hey! Who's that? Are they following us?"

Five riders were approaching at a trot. Fargo figured they had heard the shot and were curious. Then he saw who it was: Garner and the gunmen from the alley.

3

Billy Arnold recognized the horsemen a second after Fargo did. "It's them again! The ones who beat me!" Jerking the Henry to his shoulder, he tried to take a bead but Fargo wrenched the rifle from his grasp. Billy frantically tried to reclaim it but Fargo pushed against his chest, holding him back.

"Calm down, boy."

"Give me that! They followed us here! They want to finish what they started!" Desperate, Billy lunged and succeeded in wrapping his hands around the Henry's long barrel but Fargo easily tore it free again. "Do something!" Billy cried. "Shoot them or they'll shoot us!"

Fargo held the youth at arm's length, half tempted to cuff him if that was what it would take. "Take a look. They haven't touched their hardware. If they do, then, and only then, will we throw down on them."

It wasn't long before Garner reined up about ten yards out. "Look who it is. The pickpocket and the worst poker player this side of the Divide."

Pierce and a few others guffawed but not Bull Mulligan. He had a nasty bruise where Fargo had slugged him and a nasty gleam in his eyes. "I owe this bastard, Lute. Let me settle up with him." Mulligan started to climb down.

"Stay right where you are," Garner commanded.

"But there's no one else around! Who would know?"

Bull protested, and gnashed his teeth like a rabid dog anxious to attack. "All I want is five minutes! No guns, just fists. I'll pound him senseless and grind his bones to dust."

Garner twisted in the saddle, and in doing so, brushed his bearskin coat aside to reveal the nickel-plated Remington with the ivory grips, high on his right hip. "Didn't you hear me? Or maybe you reckon you'd like to take my place?"

Bull's beady eyes shifted toward the Remington and he straightened in his saddle. "You know better. Whatever you say, Lute, is always fine by me."

The bruiser's reaction told Fargo something—Lute Garner had to be greased lightning with a six-gun to inspire that kind of fear. And the others, Fargo noticed, let Mulligan flounder. They wanted no part of Garner either. "Do they fetch bones for you, too?" he remarked.

The big man in the bearskin coat leaned on his saddle horn. "Every wolf pack has a leader." He glanced at Billy, then at the buck, then at the Henry. "You've taken the runt under your wing, I gather?"

Fargo made another mental note; Lute Garner's mind was as fast as his gun hand. "Every cub has to learn sometime," he responded.

Garner laughed. He was genuinely amused, not mocking them. "True enough. I just didn't take you for the mothering type." Sobering, he looked at Billy. "Pay heed to him, boy. Learn your lessons well. Some of us stray off the straight and narrow and can never get back again no matter how hard we try." Garner touched his hat brim to Fargo, tapped his spurs against his sorrel, and led the rest off to the southwest.

Bull Mulligan glared as he went by and declared, "This isn't over, mister. We'll meet up again. You can count on it."

"Any time," Fargo said, and gave a little wave that only made Mulligan madder.

Billy was scratching his chin. "What did the one in

the bear coat mean by what he said about the straight and narrow?"

"He was being friendly."

"Him? You sure?" Billy asked dubiously. "Maybe I'm not all that old but I know a bad man when I see one. That whole bunch is trouble on the hoof, as those mule skinners would say."

Garner and company were soon out of sight. Fargo returned the Henry to its scabbard, gave the Green River skinning knife to Billy, and hunkered beside the buck. "Let's get back to work. How you skin a deer depends on whether you want to save the hide or not. If all you're after is the meat then it doesn't much matter. But we're going to save this hide so I can show you how to cure it."

"This will be awful messy." Frowning, Billy squatted beside him. "I'll get blood and gore all over me."

"It washes off."

"That's not my point. I've never done anything like this. I don't know if I can."

"You want to eat, don't you?" Fargo lifted one of the buck's rear legs. "You start by slitting the hind legs close to the knee. Then cut in a straight line from the chin to the tail, down the middle of the belly. For the front legs, slice the insides from the knees to the belly and remember to—" Fargo stopped.

The boy had gone as pale as a sheet.

Sitting back, Fargo scoured the sky for the golden eagle and spied it soaring majestically above shimmering peaks to the northwest. "See that eagle yonder?"

Billy tore his gaze from the buck. "What about it?"

"If it doesn't kill, it dies. Wolves, bears, mountain lions, coyotes, raccoons, snakes, they all kill and eat other animals. Some of them will eat you, given half the chance."

"I know that."

"Do you? Then why are you afraid to cut this deer? You're no different than that eagle or any other predator. You need to eat. In the wild you can't walk into a restaurant and order steak and potatoes. You have to fend for yourself or you die. It's that simple."

"But this poor buck," Billy said, reverently placing a hand on its neck. "It had as much right to live as we do. And I went and shot it."

Fargo sat back. This was going to take a while. "So you think everything has a 'right' to live? Do the frogs a raccoon kills have that right? Do the rabbits a coyote catches have that right? Do the deer a cougar brings down?" He encompassed the towering Rockies with a sweep of his arm. "Out here there are no rights. This is the real world, boy. It's kill or be killed. Everything is food for something else. Everything." Fargo gestured toward Denver, its tallest buildings visible on the distant horizon. "Back there it's different. We don't have to kill to eat. Or for clothes to wear. It's all handed to us. And we tend to forget the natural order of things."

"Are you saying that's wrong?"

"No. I'm saying we live in two worlds. There's the world of city life, where all our needs are met without us having to lift a finger. And there's the world of tooth and claw, where we meet our own needs. If you're not willing to do what it takes to live in both, then we might as well forget this whole idea."

Billy thoughtfully hefted the Green River knife, then clasped the buck's leg and inserted the tip. "Right about here, you said?"

For the next half hour Fargo supervised the skinning. He taught Billy how to cut the ligaments and muscles by keeping the edge of the knife toward the carcass and away from the hide to avoid marring it. He showed how to peel the hide off as if it were a long stocking being turned inside out. Then came the butchering.

Billy had to gut the buck and remove its internal organs. He wasn't too happy at first, especially when he had to reach inside and scoop out an oozing mound of intestines. But once he got over his initial revulsion, he worked with enthusiasm.

Afterward, they gathered dead brush and Fargo demonstrated how to start a fire using a fire steel and flint. Once Billy got the hang of it, he ignited pile after pile of kindling, giggling at each success. Finally, Fargo took the steel and flint, saying, "Keep this up and you're liable to burn the whole territory down."

Constructing a makeshift spit required no time at all. Billy hunkered with his forearms on his knees, watching the meat slowly roast, practically drooling at the prospect of a meal.

"When we're all done we'll pack up the rest of the meat in the hide and head back." Fargo rotated the spit so the flames licked the other side of the haunch. "You did good today, boy."

"Can you do me a favor?"

"What's that?"

"Stop calling me 'boy.' Or 'kid.' Maybe I'm not fully grown yet but I'm not a child anymore. I'm pretty near sixteen years old."

By that age, Fargo recollected, he had been on his own, making do as best he could, exactly like this wisp of a budding man. "Fair enough. From now on I'll call you Billy Goat."

Billy chuckled. "That's a good one. Just so you don't mind if I call you Old Fart."

It was Fargo's turn to laugh. He had to admit that while he still had doubts about whether he was doing the right thing, the youth showed promise. Another week or so and Billy might actually be able to live off the land without too much trouble. But that was only the first step to surviving in the wild. There was a lot more involved than knowing how to hunt and carve up game. And it was the things that a man didn't know that could easily get him killed.

During the meal they made small talk. Billy related how he had considered stowing away on a ship and learning to be a seaman but decided against a life at sea because the few times his father had taken him out in a rowboat he became sick. He told how he had spent many a night curled up in alleys with newspaper for a blanket and his own arm for a pillow.

"I had no idea what to do with my life. But I kept hearing people talk about the frontier. Gold and silver was being plucked from the ground, and new towns were springing up right and left. It got me to thinking."

"You figured to come west and make your fortune?" Fargo bit into a delicious piece of venison and sheared off a mouthful.

"No. Money's not all that important to me. It's nice to have. Don't get me wrong. But I've been without for so long that I won't lose any sleep if I don't have any." Billy gazed wistfully toward the mountains. "What I want most of all is to be my own man. To be able to get by without having to depend on anyone. To hold my head high and not be ashamed." He paused. "If that makes sense."

Mature sentiments, Fargo thought, for one so young. "Yes, it makes a lot of sense," he conceded.

Billy was unusually quiet on the ride back. As they neared the stable he brought the swayback up next to the Ovaro. "Mind if I ask you another question?"

"So long as it's not personal." Fargo meant it in jest but the youth took him seriously, and hesitated. "Go ahead. Spit it out."

"Would you say we've become friends?"

Of all the questions Fargo anticipated, that wasn't one. "Yes. I'd say we are," he said sincerely. "Why?"

"Oh, nothing." Billy beamed. "I've just never had a real friend before."

The old geezer was pacing in front of the stable, a bundle of anxiety. When he spotted them he raised his hands to the heavens as if giving thanks for the safe return of his glue bait, then spread his arms wide in greeting. "About time! You were due back an hour ago!" He saw the rolled-up hide tied across the Ovaro. "What's that you've got there?"

"Enough venison to last a month of Sundays if it's cut into strips and salted," Fargo replied. "Some of it is yours if you'll let me bed my horse another night, and the boy and me in the bargain."

The old man pursed his lips. "I sure am powerful fond of venison," he admitted. "The butcher doesn't carry it nearly as often as he used to. All anyone wants nowadays is beef."

"Do we have a deal?"

"A month of Sundays is a lot of meat." The old man thrust out his hand. "We have a deal. Oh, and before I forget, a lady stopped by earlier. Said her name was Molly and I was to give you a message." The old man scratched his head. "Now what was it again? Oh! She wants you to pay her a visit at her place along about seven. She says not to worry. That you-know-who has flown the coop and the coast is clear, whatever in tarnation that means."

Fargo was both glad and puzzled. Glad at another chance to spend a night with a luscious woman like Molly, but puzzled about the reference to her landlord flying the coop. He had another hour yet before seven, so after stripping the Ovaro and ensuring it was watered and fed, he changed into his spare buckskin shirt, tied a clean red bandanna around his throat, and brushed his boots off.

Billy was leaning against the stable door, pouting. "Are you sure I can't tag along?" he asked for the tenth or eleventh time.

"I'm sure. The old man says you can sleep in the tack room. Spread my blankets out and make yourself comfortable. I'll be back at first light. Tomorrow you learn how to track."

"I suppose a tack room is better than sleeping in an alley," Billy said sullenly.

Fargo patted him on the head and hurried down the street. He had big plans for the evening. Plans that involved more than treating himself to Molly's abundant charms. As appealing as they were, he had other priorities to attend to. And a big surprise for the kid if all went well.

Somewhere a baby was bawling when Fargo arrived at the frame house where Molly stayed. He went up the side stairs and knocked on her door. Musky perfume enveloped him as it swung open.

"Hey there, handsome. You like?"

Fargo felt a stirring in his loins. Molly had on a lacy green nightgown that clung to her like a calf-skin glove, accenting the shapely swell of her breasts and the allure of her creamy thighs. She had brushed her hair to a fine sheen, and her red lips were as inviting as cherries. "Yes," he said. "I like."

Molly grabbed his hand, pulled him inside, and sculpted her warm body to his. "I spent two hours getting ready, including an hour in the wash tub." She tittered playfully. "I'm clean enough to eat off of."

"Or eat?" Fargo kissed her, his hands roving down her arched back to her pert bottom. Her tongue met his in a sensuous swirl while her hands plied a path from the flat of his stomach to just below his belt. Caught up in the haze of his desire, Fargo almost forgot the other thing he wanted to do.

It was Molly who broke for breath and leaned back, her face flushed with lust, her bosom rising and falling to the beat of her inner craving.

"I have a favor to ask," Fargo said, hoping she wouldn't become upset with him for not whisking her off to bed right away.

"Let me guess. You want me to feed you that stew I promised?"

"No. I want you to lend me ten dollars to go play poker."

Stepping back, Molly put a hand to her throat. "Let me get this straight. I've done everything but strip my gown off and throw myself at you, and you want to run off and play cards?"

"Only for a couple of hours." That should be long

enough for Fargo to win thirty or forty dollars, if the cards weren't as cold as they had been the night before. He clasped her other hand. "You know I don't have a cent to my name. There's no other way I can get that much money quickly."

"You're forgetting something." Molly pried her hand loose. "What if you lose? You'll still be busted and I'll be out ten dollars."

"If I lose it, the next time I pass through Denver I'll pay you twenty for your trouble."

Molly clucked like an exasperated hen and slowly shook her head. "I can't believe this. I don't know whether to be insulted or mark it down to the fact you're crazy as a damn loon."

"But you'll do it?"

A smile crept across her lovely face. "Lord help me. I must be as crazy as you are. I'll lend you the money. But on two conditions. First, you have to be back in my arms by nine o'clock, not a minute later."

"And the second condition?"

Molly's smile widened. "You're mine for the rest of the night. No ifs, ands, or buts about it." She walked to an oak table and picked up her handbag.

"What happened to your landlord?" Fargo remembered to ask.

"He left me a note saying he had to go out of town for a few days and asked me to look after the place while he's gone." Molly fished out several bills. "Lucky for us."

"Has he ever gone away like this before?"

"No. What difference does it make? He's gone and we can do as we please until the cock crows." Molly impishly glanced at his groin. "Or grows, if you get my drift." She brought over the ten dollars. "Here you go. Reckon I'll sit around twiddling my thumbs until you get back."

Fargo kissed her again, this time sucking on her tongue while kneading her thighs. Her legs grew weak and she leaned against him, mewing like a kitten.

"I want you so damn much."

"I'm sorry." With that, Fargo was out the door before his own hunger betrayed him. The truth was, he wanted her just as much. The image of her shimmery gown clinging to her voluptuous contours haunted him all the way to the nearest saloon.

It was early yet, but a couple of poker games were in progress. Fargo claimed an empty chair at a table with three other players. Two were middle-aged townsmen, the third a grungy prospector with more money than sense. In half an hour Fargo was up twelve dollars, but it was nowhere near enough.

The prospector kept up an endless prattle. About the latest gold strikes. About the weather. About the cost of beans. And then he made a comment that piqued everyone's interest.

"It's a cryin' shame about those fellers the Utes wiped out last week, ain't it? I hope the army catches the red devils responsible and strings 'em up good and proper."

"Four men were massacred, they say," a townsman commented.

This was the first Fargo had heard of the Utes acting up, and it was news worth knowing. He traveled through their territory frequently. "Why did the Utes do it?" The tribe was generally peaceful despite continued white encroachment.

"Who the hell knows, sonny?" was the prospector's reply. "There's no explainin' Injuns. This is the third time those bloodthirsty heathens have struck in the past several months. They always mutilate the bodies and steal everything they can get their hands on, includin' the clothes off their victims' backs."

"That's strange," Fargo remarked. Unlike the Apaches, the Utes didn't make it a habit to carve up enemies. Usually they killed them outright. And while in the past the tribe had been known to steal a few horses and guns, stealing clothes was unheard of. Especially clothes off the dead. "What makes the army think the Utes are to blame?"

"The Utes are the only Injuns in these parts, aren't they?" the prospector rejoined. "And they're so dumb, they've left broken arrows and whatnot behind. If you ask me, there ain't an Injun born with half the brains of a white man."

Fargo suddenly felt an intense urge to win every dollar the prospector had. He never liked bigots, but he had to be careful not to give his feelings away and, above all, not to let his anger spoil his play.

A townsman was dealing. "One of the victims was chopped to bits, I heard. The pieces were as small as peas."

"It just proves what everyone has been sayin' for ages," the prospector said. "The only good Injun is a dead Injun."

Fargo refrained from revealing that he had lived with Indians on occasion, and that he'd met many who were as decent as the year was long. He buckled down to the game. The hand he was dealt wasn't good enough to open but one of the other players did, and Fargo asked for three cards. He ended up with two pair, kings and jacks. It proved good enough to win the pot. The next hand, he was dealt strays and folded, but on the hand after that he was given a seven, eight, and nine of various suits, a jack of hearts, and an ace of spades. Logic dictated he get rid of the lower cards and hold on to the jack and the ace in the hope of acquiring a pair of one or the other. Instead, he discarded the ace.

"You want just one?" The prospector grinned, showing a gap where two upper front teeth had been. "You must think you have a mighty good hand."

His face cast in iron, Fargo slowly raised the card he'd been dealt. The odds of getting a straight were formidable. But there it was, the ten he needed.

"I have a pretty good hand myself," the prospector was saying. "Enough to go the limit."

Fargo stayed in. A flush, a full house, four of a kind, a straight flush, a royal flush—any could beat his hand. But he was playing a hunch. He had a feeling the prospector was bluffing, and if he was right, he stood to rake in the biggest pot yet.

One of the townsmen stayed in the game until the very last, and laid out two pair, deuces and fours. Fargo showed his straight. That left the prospector, who took his sweet time laying down a pair of sixes.

"Oh well. Sometimes a bluff works, sometimes it doesn't. A man doesn't know until he tries."

Fargo had discovered a long time ago that poor poker players had an unending supply of excuses for why they lost. Most boiled down to bad luck. But random chance wasn't the only factor in the game. A lot of skill went into it. Foremost was the ability to read the cards as well as the other players. It separated professional gamblers from the sheep they fleeced. And while Fargo didn't rate himself a professional, he was better than most.

Raking in his winnings, Fargo debated whether to keep playing. He had won close to forty dollars. Another ten would be nice to have. But a warm and willing woman was impatiently waiting to rip his clothes off, and who was he to keep her waiting? "Thanks for the game, gents."

The sun had long since set and the streets were filling with Denver's nocturnal denizens. Fargo passed more than a dozen women in tight dresses brazenly flaunting their wares. One blocked his path and asked him to step into a nearby alley, but he declined and moved on.

A lamp glowed in Molly's window. Smiling in anticipation, Fargo came to the bottom of the steps and had just lifted his right foot when four shadows detached themselves from the surrounding darkness and pounced. He grabbed for his Colt but iron arms looped around him from the rear. He butted backward with his head and was rewarded with a grunt, but the man didn't let go and the next moment a fist caught him on the jaw.

Fighting to stay conscious, Fargo was vaguely aware of being carted up the stairs, of the door opening, of being flung on the carpet and having the Colt snatched from its holster. He was also aware of low laughter.

"We meet again, bumpkin. Only this time the shoe is on the other foot."

Matt Dirkson was on the settee, one arm draped around Molly. She had a bruise on her chin and her nightgown was ripped at the shoulder.

"I'm sorry, Skye. He said he would break my arm if I tried to warn you."

Fargo rose onto his hands and knees. The four men ringing him were dollar-an-hour slabs of hired muscle. One had shoved the Colt under his own belt. "Let Molly go. This doesn't concern her."

"I beg to differ," Dirkson responded. "She witnessed my humiliation last night, so it's only fair she witness yours. And who knows? If she pleads and begs, I might even let her visit you in the hospital."

4

Skye Fargo's eagerness to savor Molly's charms was to blame for his predicament. Had he been more alert when he arrived, he wouldn't have been taken by surprise. Now, as the four men prepared to do Dirkson's bidding, he tried a bluff. "Go ahead. Start something. Her landlord will have the marshal here before you know it."

Matt Dirkson chuckled. "Tell him, my dear." He smugly ran a hand down Molly's arm. "Fill the bumpkin in on my brilliant little deception."

"My landlord isn't out of town like I thought," Molly said. "He's still in Denver, over at the Imperial Hotel. Matt paid him a hundred and fifty dollars. All so he can get back at you for the beating you gave him."

"Exactly. And it will be worth every cent," Dirkson crowed. He tried to stroke her chin but she pulled away. "Now, now. Let's not be childish. After I'm done with him, you and I are having a long talk about our future."

"There's nothing to talk about." Molly attempted to rise but Dirkson yanked her back down. Furious, she slapped his hand, but all he did was laugh. "I warn you, Matt. Harm a hair on his head and I'll go to the marshal myself."

"Be my guest. I'll say your friend assaulted me without provocation and these four men came to my assistance." Dirkson sniffed her hair. "Which one of us do you think the marshal will believe? The vice president of a prestigious bank and a pillar of the community? Or a saloon tart whose morals are less than sterling?"

Swearing luridly, Molly attempted to slap him but Dirkson caught her wrist and twisted it sharply, causing her to cry out.

"Behave yourself, my dear, or you won't like the consequences."

Fargo was being ignored. The four toughs were staring at Dirkson and Molly, not at him. Consequently, no one saw him lift his right boot high enough to ease his right hand under his pant leg and grip the hilt of the Arkansas Toothpick he always kept snug in an ankle sheath. Before he could pull it out, heavy hands fell on his shoulders and he was snapped upright. Both his arms were seized by fingers of stone.

Matt Dirkson slowly rose, a cat about to swallow a canary. "Hold him good and tight, gentlemen."

"No!" Molly flung herself off the settee and clutched at Dirkson's jacket. "Please, Matt! Let him go and I'll do whatever you want."

A change came over Dirkson, a transformation so abrupt, so violent, Molly stepped back in fear. His smile vanished, to be replaced by a feral snarl. A mask of sheer savagery contorted his face as, gripping her by the hair, he twisted her head to one side. "You'll do what I want *anyway*! Never forget that!" Shoving her, he planted himself in front of Fargo and bunched his fists.

The two men holding Fargo firmed their grips. The other two moved out of the way to give the banker room.

"I'm going to enjoy the hell out of this," Dirkson said.

"Think so?" Fargo kneed him where it always hurt a man most. A screech tore from Dirkson's throat and he tottered back, his hands thrown protectively over his privates. Sputtering and wheezing, he doubled over, which put his chin right where Fargo wanted it.

Fargo kicked him in the face, sending Dirkson stumbling into the settee. The men on either side were caught flat-footed. Their first instinct was to hold him fast but he was too quick. He slammed a boot against one man's knee, rotated, and drove an elbow into the gut of the second.

The others closed in but Fargo was ready. The crunch of his knuckles against a nose was music to his ears. A right cross drove the fourth man back. And then Fargo was striking right and left, smashing anyone who tried to land a blow. Three of his adversaries were down, dazed and bleeding, when the fourth one bellowed like a mad moose and leaped in again, his arms outstretched.

Fargo met him with an uppercut that bent his attacker like a bow. In a blur, he snatched the Colt, sprang well to one side, and cocked the hammer.

To a man, the quartet mimicked ice sculptures.

Matt Dirkson was on his knees, his face the color of a plum, puffing like a winded horse. "What are you waiting for?" he croaked at his gunnies. "Get the son of a bitch!"

"Not me," one said, shaking his head. "I don't have a hankering to die."

"We know when we're licked," said another, dabbing a sleeve at blood on his mouth. "All we want is to mosey on our way."

Fargo gave them added incentive. "If you're not out that door by the time I count to five, you'll take lead anyway." He got to three. The clomp of their boots faded into the night, and he walked over to Matt Dirkson and jammed the Colt's muzzle against Dirkson's ear.

The banker withered like a dying plant and shrieked, "You can't! It would be murder! They'll hunt you down and hang you!"

Fargo raised the revolver to slam the barrel against Dirkson's head but Molly beat him to it. Out of nowhere she brought a frying pan crashing down, hitting Dirkson again and again and again. The banker sprawled onto his stomach. With blood flowing from his scalp, he weakly fought against her onslaught.

"Enough," Fargo said, catching her by the waist and pulling her away. "Keep it up and you'll kill him."

Livid beyond measure, Molly struggled like a she-cat in a net. "What do you think I'm trying to do? Let me go! He has this coming!"

It was all Fargo could do to hold her. "He's not worth a stretch in prison," he observed. "Throw him down the stairs if you want, but get rid of the pan." He never intended for her to take him seriously but damned if she didn't toss the pan to the floor, grip Dirkson by the shoulders, and drag him out the door. Dirkson resisted but he was too befuddled to do more than pry at her fingers, and moments later she had him on the landing.

Fargo followed and scoured the yard for the thugs, but they were gone.

There was a thud and a screech and he turned in time to see Matt Dirkson tumble head over heels to the bottom of the stairs and lie in an inert heap, one leg bent at an angle legs weren't meant to bend.

Molly was flushed, her hair disheveled, her nightgown askew. Yet she had never looked more beautiful. "I swear to God if he ever shows up here again, I'll kill the slug."

Fargo touched her shoulder and she whirled. For a second he thought she would tear into him, too. Instead, she threw her arms around his neck and he felt tears moisten his skin.

"Thank you, Skye."

"You're the one who tossed him out on his ear," Fargo joked. He was trying to make her smile but she began weeping in great racking sobs. He held her close to console her and couldn't help but be distracted by the feel of her full breasts against his chest and the clinging warmth of her thighs on his. A lump formed in his throat and he had to cough to relieve it.

At length Molly stepped back, sniffling. "Give me a few minutes to touch up," she said, and darted inside.

"There's whiskey in the cabinet," she threw over a shoulder.

Fargo dispensed with a glass. Opening the bottle, he chugged several times, then sat on the settee with his boots propped on a low table, careful not to scratch it with his spurs. He hadn't said anything to Molly but he was concerned for her safety. Matt Dirkson wasn't the kind to forgive and forget; the beating he'd taken would only fuel his rage. Fargo wouldn't put it past him to return when Molly least expected it and cause her more grief.

Rising, Fargo went out onto the landing. He took it for granted the banker would still be lying at the bottom, but Dirkson was gone! Taking the steps three at a bound, Fargo quickly reached the ground. He searched the yard from end to end but it was empty. Either Dirkson hadn't been as hurt as he seemed, or the gunnies had come back for him.

Returning to the landing, Fargo took another swig of rotgut. Before he left Denver, he must look Dirkson up and persuade him to leave Molly alone.

To be on the safe side, Fargo bolted the door. Humming came from the bedroom. Molly was in fine spirits; she thought the worst was over. Fargo decided not to disabuse her of the notion just yet. In the morning would do.

The bedroom door opened. In a swirl of lace and perfume, Molly crossed the room and fused herself to him. She had switched to a blue nightgown every bit as sheer and skimpy as the green one. Satiny smooth to the touch, it was cut so low in front, it barely covered her nipples.

"See anything you like, handsome?"

"That lamp on the table is nice," Fargo quipped, and received a light punch on the arm.

Molly ground herself against him and bit his chin. "You know what I mean, you ornery devil!"

Lips that tasted like ripe strawberries rose to meet Fargo's, and a tongue as smooth as silk danced with his.

The kiss lingered on and on, Molly squirming with antici- pation. Fargo massaged her back in small circles from her shoulder blades to her hips.

"Mmmmmm. You really know how to kiss." Molly com- plimented him when at long last they broke for breath.

"Beginner's luck."

Molly snorted. "Bull. Something tells me you've been with more gals than I could count. Not that I mind." She flicked the tip of her tongue across his right cheek. "A lot of men can't kiss worth a damn. They think they have to be rough. Or else they don't like to use their tongue."

"Practice makes perfect." Again Fargo glued his mouth to hers and drew her toward the settee. Side by side, they sank down. Fargo stroked her hair, then plied his fingers lower. She seemed fascinated by the corded sinews on his arms and chest. Tugging on his shirt, she slipped a hand up under it.

"Oh my. Your stomach is like a washboard," Molly mentioned lightheartedly. "Even your muscles have muscles."

Fargo ran his left hand up over her thigh to the flat of her stomach. She quivered at his touch. A low mew escaped her as he roved higher to cup a full breast. Her nipple was hard against his palm. He tweaked it between a forefinger and thumb, and she gasped and wriggled.

"If you get me any hotter I'll ravish you."

"Promises, promises," Fargo teased, and received a kiss that sent a tingle clear down to his toes. Her lips were exquisitely soft, her tongue molten fire. She was panting heavily when next they drew back.

"I want you."

The feeling was mutual. Fargo held her close and squeezed each of her breasts in turn, hard enough to elicit a low cry. Bending, he nuzzled her ripe melons, nosed her nightgown lower, and applied his mouth to an inviting tip.

"Ohhhhh." Molly dug her fingernails into his biceps, her rosy mouth forming a delectable oval. "I like that."

Fargo inhaled her nipple, rimming it with his tongue, then flicked it several times. One of her hands strayed to his head, knocking his hat off, and she gripped his hair with all her might, as if seeking to tear it out by the roots. He slid a hand between her legs, intending to stroke her core, but she abruptly went weak at the knees. To keep her from falling, he had to scoop her into his arms.

"The bedroom," Molly whispered in his ear, and ran her tongue along its edge, stopping to suck the lobe.

A sturdy four-poster bed awaited, the quilt already thrown back. Fargo gently deposited her on her back, her head on a pillow. She tried to pull him down on top of her but he said, "Wait." As swiftly as possible he removed his boots, his gunbelt, and his shirt.

Smiling seductively, Molly slid out of her nightgown. In the golden glow of a lamp on the dresser she was beauty personified. Her luxurious hair, the splendor of her naked body, the upward thrust of her twin globes were captivating. Fargo kissed her navel and slowly worked higher, covering every square inch of skin.

Languidly stretching her arms above her head, Molly said softly, "If the other girls at the saloon knew about you, they'd line up to take turns."

Fargo clamped his mouth on a nipple. Her legs parted and her ankles locked behind his hips. She was getting a little ahead of herself but that was fine by him. Kneading her other breast, he pressed a knee against her nether mound. She was a furnace down there. His knee grew moist as the room filled with a musky female scent.

Not until her breasts were heaving and she was squirming uncontrollably did Fargo slide higher and place his mouth on hers. She sucked on his tongue for long, sensuous minutes, her hands always in motion. His own breath grew hot as she undid his belt and loosened his pants sufficiently for her to slide a hand down in. At the touch of her fingers on his manhood, Fargo couldn't suppress

46

a groan. She fondled him from top to bottom and back up again, then cupped him, low down.

Another lump formed in Fargo's throat. His skin prickled as if from a heat rash. Molly pushed him onto his knees, wriggled into a sitting position, and exposed his pole in all its rigid glory.

"You're a regular stallion," Molly said huskily, and eased down.

Fargo closed his eyes, rested his hands on her head, and let himself drift on a sea of velvet ecstasy. A few lingering tendrils of tension drained from him like water from a sieve. Time and place lost all meaning. There was only the wonderfully moist sensation of her mouth and tongue. He would have been content to kneel there forever if not for the explosion slowly building deep inside him. To thwart it, he eased her onto her back and dallied at her breasts until he had himself under control.

Molly grew impatient. "Now, lover. Now."

Fargo spread her legs wider. Gripping his member, he ran it along her wet slit, sparking a shiver. But he didn't enter her just yet.

"What are you waiting for?" Molly complained. She reached for him. "Do I have to draw you a map?"

Grinning, Fargo aligned his manhood with her sheath. She pushed against him with her heels but he refused to be rushed. Inch by gradual inch he fed himself into her, savoring the silken cling of her inner walls. Molly held herself perfectly still, eyes shut. The instant he was buried to the hilt, she cried out and dug her nails into his shoulders deep enough to draw blood. Almost before he could set himself, she bucked like a wild mustang and would have hurled him halfway across the room if not for the vise-like grip of her legs around his waist.

"Do it to me, big man! Do me hard!"

Fargo had other ideas. He pumped slowly, his hands busy everywhere.

Heedless of the pace he was setting, Molly flung herself against him in urgent abandon. She was eager for release, with or without him. Faster and faster she went, until, throwing back her head and biting her lower lip, she spurted like a geyser. A loud moan filled the bedroom, a moan that went on and on, ending with a long-drawn, "Yessssssssss." Molly collapsed, spent and perspiring, then realized he was still rocking back and forth. "Ohhh my!"

Gripping her hips, Fargo drove up into her with the force of a battering ram. It brought her up off the bed with her eyes wide and her mouth agape. For a moment he had the illusion she was suspended in midair. Then her arms hooked around his shoulders and she clung to him as if for dear life.

"More! More! More!"

Fargo gave her what she wanted, and then some. He held out as long as he could, delaying the inevitable through sheer willpower until there came a moment when his body would no longer be denied. He crested. Waves of physical rapture rippled over, through, and around him. He lost himself in the bliss. In the sensation that, for a while at least, all was right with the world.

Eventually the haze of climax faded, as it always did. Fargo drifted down from the lofty heights of pleasure to the reality of sweaty lassitude. He became conscious of his heart beating in his chest, of pain in his shoulders and arms where Molly had scratched and clawed like a wildcat.

"You're magnificent," she cooed, tracing his left eyebrow with a fingertip.

"I'm tired." Rolling onto his side, Fargo draped an arm across her bosom. Drowsiness weighed him down like an anchor. He was asleep almost instantly. Barely a minute later, or so it seemed, loud knocking on the front door snatched him from slumber, and he slowly rose up onto his elbows.

"What's that?" Molly sleepily muttered, struggling to

sit up. "I'm not expecting anyone. Who can it be at this late hour?"

"I have a fair notion." Fargo wouldn't put it past Matt Dirkson to sic the law on them. Sliding out of the bed, he dressed, strapped his gunbelt on, and hastened into the next room. "Who the hell is it?" he demanded.

A man shouted something Fargo couldn't quite make out. His hand on the Colt, he cautiously moved nearer and repeated his question.

"Sorry to disturb you. I'm Captain Luther Parmenton. I was told I could find a scout by the name of Skye Fargo here. Would you happen to be him?"

Fargo wasn't taking chances. Gripping the latch, he drew his revolver, then swung the door wide.

A young officer in a dusty uniform, about to knock again, turned into marble. "I knew I should have waited until tomorrow," he blurted. Below him on the steps stood a sergeant with a thick mustache and a private as skinny as a rake. "You are the gentleman in question, I take it?"

Nodding, Fargo replaced the Colt. "Captain Parmenton, is it? Who told you where to find me?"

"A kid at the stable on the north side of town. Billy Arnold. We've been looking for you for three days now, asking all over the place. It's just pure luck we stumbled onto him." Parmenton was going to say more but a look of utter astonishment came over him and he whisked his hat off his head as if it were on fire. "How do you do, ma'am?"

A hand fell on Fargo's shoulder. He hadn't heard Molly come up in her bare feet. She had thrown on a robe, but it hung half open, exposing enough to get her arrested if she went out in public.

"Friends of yours, handsome?"

The sergeant and the private doffed their caps, the former trying hard not to gawk at her breasts and failing, the latter appearing ready to bolt if she so much as winked in his direction.

"I never saw them before." And Fargo wasn't all that pleased to make their acquaintance at that particular moment. Whenever the army sent a special detail to find him, it invariably spelled trouble.

"Where are our manners?" Molly said, and moved aside. "Make yourselves comfortable, gentlemen, and I'll throw some coffee on the stove."

The sergeant bolted forward like a Thoroughbred out of the starting gate but Captain Parmenton thrust an arm in front of him. "That won't be necessary, ma'am. I wouldn't think of imposing. We'll make arrangements to meet Mr. Fargo tomorrow and be on our way."

That was fine by Fargo but Molly wanted to play hostess.

"Nonsense, Captain. Never let it be said I can't be as hospitable as the next person. You and your men have a seat on the settee. I won't be long." Molly waltzed toward the stove, her posterior swaying saucily.

Fargo claimed the rocking chair. Since there was no avoiding it, he intended to find out why they were there and whisk them on their way. "I'm all ears, Captain."

Parmenton sat as stiff-backed as a West Point cadet. "I'm terribly sorry to have barged in on you like this. That is, I mean, well, you know what I mean." He toyed with his hat to cover his unease.

"You said you were looking for me?" Fargo spurred him along.

"Yes, sir. Under orders from Colonel Tananbaum. Commanding officer at Fort Wise. Word reached him you were in the territory and he dispatched several search parties to find you."

Fargo had been to Fort Wise before but never met Tananbaum. Originally called Fort Fauntleroy, it was renamed for reasons that eluded everyone but the army. Located not far from Bent's Fort on a bank of the Arkansas River, the post was intended to protect settlers moving into the region and to ensure mail and stage service wasn't interrupted by hostiles.

"Have you heard about the Ute uprising?" the captain inquired.

Fargo wouldn't call three attacks an "uprising," and said so.

"There have been five attacks to date, sir, not just three. And seventeen people have lost their lives. The last incident was a week and a half ago not twenty-five miles southwest of where we sit. One of the victims was a woman barely twenty years old. The colonel is worried civilians might take it into their heads to burn down a few Ute villages in revenge, so he's hushed it up so far."

With valid cause, Fargo mused. Whenever a few warriors stepped out of line, a lot of other innocent Indians suffered.

"We've tried our best to track the culprits down," the young captain continued. "The colonel even hired a couple of Arapahos who could supposedly track a flea across solid rock but they went off into the mountains and never came back."

"Warriors don't just disappear," Fargo said.

Parmenton perched his hat on his knees but it fell and he had to grab it. "I agree, sir. But no one has come across hide nor hair of them. It's the darnedest thing."

"And by now your colonel is at his wit's end and wants me to try my hand at doing what no one else has been able to?" Fargo guessed.

"That's pretty much the gist of why I'm here, yes, sir. Colonel Tananbaum asked around. He sent queries to other forts. And everyone said the same thing." Captain Parmenton paused. "They say you're the best there is at what you do. They say you're the best tracker alive, maybe the best who ever lived. The colonel is convinced that if anyone has a chance of finding the Ute war party and putting an end to the bloodshed, you're the man for the job." Parmenton paused again. "What do you say? Can I let the colonel know you've agreed?"

"Hell," Fargo said. Not because he resented being asked. But because he knew what he would say before the question was broached, knew it as surely as he knew himself and his damnable conscience.

"Sir?" Parmenton said.

"I'll head out first thing in the morning."

5

Skye Fargo was about five miles southwest of Denver when he discovered he was being followed. He was winding through rolling foothills toward the high peaks. He came to the crest of one of the highest and glanced over his shoulder to check his back trail. It was a habit, as ingrained as breathing, and it had saved his hide more times than he could recollect. In this instance, he took one look and stiffened in the saddle.

Someone was shadowing him. Half a mile back was another rider, keeping to the same pace he was. It might be a coincidence. It could merely be someone bound for the gold fields. Then again, it could also mean trouble.

The merest touch of Fargo's spurs sent the pinto over the hill at a trot. Once out of sight of the shadow rider, he reined sharply to the right, into a stand of evergreens, and dismounted. Sliding the Henry from its scabbard, he crouched behind a tree close to the trail and waited.

Soon the clomp of hooves preceded the appearance of a rider at the top of the hill.

Fargo automatically snapped the Henry to his shoulder, and just as quickly lowered it again. "I'll be damned." Anger carried him out into the middle of the trail where he faced his follower and loudly demanded, "Just what in hell do you think you're doing?"

Billy Arnold reined up. "What does it look like?" he rejoined defensively. "I'm tagging along."

"I told you to stay in Denver." Fargo stalked to the swayback and grabbed the bridle. "I told you to stay at the stable and cut up that venison. And to find yourself some new clothes—" Fargo stopped as what he was seeing sank in. The boy *had* bought new clothes; buckskins exactly like his, a red bandanna identical to his, a hat similar to his, and boots the exact same style and color. A new Colt was strapped around the kid's waist. It was like looking at a mirror image of himself, only years younger and a hundred pounds lighter. "What in God's name did you do?"

"Do you like it?" Billy smiled proudly. "I had to race around like an antelope to buy everything in time so I could head out and catch up before you got too much of a lead on me."

"You bought the swayback?"

Billy's smile widened. "The old man at the stable gave me a great deal. Since I'd used up most of the money you gave me on my new clothes and gun, he let me have the horse for the venison. An even swap, just because he likes me so much. Wasn't that decent of him?"

Considering the nag was just about the sorriest excuse for a horse Fargo ever saw, the liveryman clearly got the better of the deal. "Why didn't you buy clothes that *you* like? Why copy me?"

"Because I want to be just like you," Billy confessed. "I've been practicing walking like you, talking like you. Why, once I put some pounds on me, people won't be able to tell the difference."

Fargo didn't know what to say. It was flattering, he supposed. But it was also downright spooky.

"Why?" Billy continued. "What's wrong? You're the first real friend I've had since my parents died." When Fargo didn't say anything, more poured from Billy in a torrent. "I want to be just like you. I want to learn everything you know and become a scout and do all the things you do. That's why I followed you. And before you say anything, yes, I know I didn't listen. But I can't wait to learn more. You promised to teach me to track and I aim to hold you to it." Billy added almost as an afterthought, "Haven't you ever had anyone look up to you before?"

"Not like this." And it made Fargo uncomfortable. "Listen, it's nice you think so highly of me. But you should do things the way you like to do them, not the way I like to. You're not me. You're *you*. As for following me, I thought I made it clear I'm going after a band of renegades. It's too dangerous for you to come along."

Billy thrust out his lower lip. "So? Danger is part and parcel of a scout's life. You said so yourself. Besides, I'm not stupid. I'll make myself scarce once arrows start to fly."

"No. And that's final." Fargo let go of the bridle.

Billy's features hardened. "I won't go back and you can't make me. I don't care what you say. I'll keep dogging you for as long as it takes to get you to see things my way."

Fargo came close to dumping the youth to the ground. But that wouldn't accomplish anything other than to make Billy more angry. To buy himself time to think, Fargo retrieved the Ovaro, replaced the Henry, and forked leather. "I'm not going to waste my breath arguing. If you want me to teach you the skills you need to survive in the wild, then you have to do as I tell you."

Billy sat sullenly a few moments, then brought the swayback up next to the Ovaro. "The only way you can stop me is to shoot me."

Fargo disliked being sassed. He reminded himself that Billy's assertions to the contrary, Billy was still a kid. And kids Billy's age were notorious for being as stubborn as mules. "I could drag you back by the scruff of your neck."

"But you won't," Billy said confidently. "You would lose too much time. The army needs the Utes found before more people are killed."

The kid had a point, Fargo conceded. Captain Parmenton had given him explicit directions to the spot where the last attack took place, and it would take over a day to get there. If he took Billy back, it would be two days unless he rode all night. And he would rather be well rested when he set out after the Utes. "You have it all thought out, don't you?"

"You're the one who told me a good scout always thinks things out ahead." Billy threw his own words at him. "I'm not doing this just to be mean. Not after all you've done for me. Next to my father, I think you're the greatest man who ever lived."

Fargo was beginning to think he was the dumbest. His poker winnings had been enough for new duds and whatnot, with a little left to tide the boy over until he got back. It never occurred to him that Billy would trade the venison for the nag. "If I ever see that old buzzard at the stable again, I'm going to dunk him in the horse trough."

"What for? He was kind enough to throw in this saddle for free." Billy patted the cracked horn. The saddle itself looked as if it was held together by spit and bailing wire. "If you ask me, I got the better of the deal."

"I can see it's time for another lesson. People who treat you kindly don't always have your best interests at heart. Sometimes they're up to no good. You have to learn to read people like you do animals and tracks or they'll be forever taking advantage of you." Resigned to the inevitable, Fargo rode on and didn't object when his mirror image caught up.

"How do you read a person?" the questions began.

"By letting their actions speak for them. They might say one thing and mean another, or be lying through their teeth. The Indians call it talking with two tongues or a forked tongue."

"So you're saying I should never trust anyone at first sight? Even a minister or a baby in a carriage?"

The boy asked the damnedest things. Fargo wondered if this was what parents went through all the time. "Did you hear me say that? Give others the benefit of the doubt but never take anything for granted. Trust must be earned. Only then can you let down your guard."

On they rode, Billy plying him with query after query, Fargo answering as best he was able. Over an hour had gone by when Billy slyly grinned and mentioned, "I guess you're not sending me back, huh?"

Fargo was certain the kid wouldn't stay put if he did. In his estimation it was smarter to keep Billy close where he could keep an eye on him, and out of mischief. "You're to do exactly as I say at all times. Buck me once more, for any reason, and I'm through teaching you. Savvy?"

"You can count on me," Billy said with a straight face.

By evening they were well into the Rockies, camped in a clearing along the trail. Fargo shot a rabbit and had Billy butcher it. He also had Billy kindle their fire, fetch water from a stream, and set stew on to boil.

"It must be nice having your own personal slave," the boy grumbled as he stirred the pot.

"Out here a man learns by doing. The more he does something, the better he is at it." Fargo was stretched out on his blankets, his back propped against his saddle. "So get used to the idea of cooking our supper from now until the cows come home. Or head back to Denver and take up picking pockets again."

Billy wisely changed the subject. "Tell me more about the animals and their habits."

Until almost midnight they stayed up talking, Fargo imparting knowledge to his attentive student. When various creatures were most active, where they liked to hole up, what they ate, how often they slaked their thirst, and much more. Billy absorbed it all, his curiosity boundless. By the time they turned in, Fargo's throat was raw from so much gabbing. He wasn't used to it.

"Shouldn't one of us stand guard?" was the last question of the day.

"My horse will whinny if anything comes around. But

if it will make you feel safer, you can always stuff branches and rocks under your blanket and go sleep in the bushes." Fargo used the ruse on occasion but he didn't deem it warranted now. The Ute war party was likely long gone, back to any one of half a dozen villages far to the southwest.

"If you're brave enough to sleep in the open, I am, too," Billy informed him.

It had been a long day. Fargo was soon about to drift off. The last thing he heard was his pupil's marveling voice.

"Sakes alive! Look at all those stars. I never saw so many, not even out on the prairie. They're so close, you can practically reach out and touch them!" A contented sigh wafted across the clearing. "Yes, sir. This sure is the life for me."

Smiling, Fargo fell asleep. Twice during the night he was awakened when Billy thrashed about and mumbled to himself. Bad dreams, Fargo figured, and didn't disturb him.

Faint shades of pink suffused the eastern sky when Fargo awoke and put coffee on. He deliberately made a lot more noise than he ordinarily would, but Billy Arnold slumbered on, oblivious to the world around him. Filling a tin cup with water, Fargo upended it over the boy's face and stepped back as Billy came up sputtering and yowling.

"What the hell is going on?" As riled as a wet hen, Billy mopped a sleeve across his face. On spying Fargo and the tin cup he put two and two together. "It was you? Why couldn't you just give me a shake or something?"

"You're a heavy sleeper." Fargo stepped to his bedding to roll it up.

"I know I am. What's that got to do with anything?" Billy's cheeks and chin were still damp and he wiped his other sleeve across them.

Fargo removed a twig that had fallen on his blanket

58

during the night. "Out here heavy sleepers die young. Train yourself to wake up at the slightest strange sound."

"How am I supposed to do that when practically everything I hear out here is strange?" Billy countered.

"It takes time." As it had with Fargo. The first night he ever heard wolves howl, he had sat up until morning in fear of being attacked.

"More of that practice makes perfect stuff, huh?" Billy jammed his hat on and stood. "Well, if I don't learn, it won't be for lack of trying. I've never wanted anything so much in my life as to be a scout."

Before the sun crowned the eastern horizon they were in the saddle and pushing steadily southwest. Toward the middle of the morning they left the main trail and took a side trail that meandered into a remote region where a new mining camp had recently sprung up.

The site of the latest attack wasn't hard to find. There had been five whites in the party, three on horseback and a man and woman on a wagon. The army had learned they were on their way to Denver to convert gold ore they had unearthed into cash money. They never made it.

On a narrow switchback bordered by a steep open slope on one side and a sheer drop-off on the other, the Utes had struck with ruthless efficiency. The men on horseback were blasted from their saddles before they knew what hit them. The wagon was brought to a halt, the couple were dragged off and slain. While some of the Utes helped themselves to the gold ore, the rest mutilated the bodies. Their last act before riding off was to set the wagon ablaze.

Or so the official version had it.

Fargo had entertained doubts when Captain Parmenton told him the story, and now, as he sat astride the Ovaro scouring the switchback, his doubts resurfaced. There was no cover anywhere. No one could approach within fifty or sixty yards without being seen. It was as poor a spot for an ambush as he had ever seen, and any

Ute would think the same. He mentioned his observation to Billy.

"Maybe the Indians rushed them from above and below at same time," the boy speculated.

Fargo couldn't see that happening, either. The stretch of trail above and below the switchback was too exposed. The Utes would be picked off. He pointed this out. "It would be stupid to attack here. And Indians aren't stupid." He kneed the stallion closer. "No, the reason the attackers were able to get so close to the prospectors had to be because the prospectors had no reason to suspect they were in danger."

Billy mulled that over. "Are you saying the attackers were white?"

"Could be."

"But white men don't carve up other whites."

"They do if they want Indians to take the blame." Fargo rode off the trail to the charred remains of the wagon. Its bed and sides were gone but most of the axle and gear were intact. The ground around it had been churned by hooves and overlaid with footprints left by the cavalry and others who had happened by since. To find the tracks of the attackers would be the proverbial needle in a haystack.

Billy was thinking the same thing. "How the army expects you to hunt down the killers after all this time is beyond me. Any tracks they made have all been erased."

"Maybe not." Fargo wheeled the Ovaro and headed back down. Whoever stole the gold would want to get out of there as quickly as possible. They wouldn't push on to the mining camp and risk running into someone who could place them on the trail at the time of the attack. They had to have gone back down the mountain.

At the junction Fargo drew rein to ponder. To the right, the main trail wound off toward more camps and distant settlements. To the left it led to Denver. The bandits had two options. Both entailed the same risk of being seen. To make their problem worse, all that ore would slow them down.

"Which way do you think they went?" Billy asked.

"Neither." Fargo slapped his legs against the pinto and rode straight across the trail and into the woods on the other side. The way he saw it, the bandits needed four or five pack animals to transport that much ore. Since they didn't dare dispose of it right after the killings, they had to lay low for a while. Hide out with their animals and their ill-gotten gains until the uproar died down. Only this time there hadn't been an uproar because the army clamped a lid on the attack. But they didn't know that, so they must still be in hiding.

"You sure are a puzzlement," Billy said. "What do you expect to find in this forest? Pinecones?"

Again Fargo reined up. He pointed to a set of prints vaguely defined in the carpet of pine needles. "Notice anything about those tracks that's different from those of our own horses?"

Billy scratched the peach fuzz on his bony chin. "Give me a minute." Sliding down, he dropped onto his hands and knees and examined the tracks with great care. "These are deeper," he said. He glanced up. "That means the horses that made them were carrying heavy loads! The ore!"

"Well done."

"But they're not shod. And I thought only Indian horses went without shoes?"

"Figure it out," Fargo prompted.

Billy snapped his fingers. "Someone removed the shoes to make everyone think it was Utes!"

"We'll know soon enough." The killers had stuck to heavy timber for several miles. Fargo counted five pack animals, seven riders.

A little further down the trail Fargo came upon a new set of hoofprints that complicated matters. Five riders had come in from the southwest, paralleled the tracks of the ambushers for a short distance, then veered northeast toward Denver. And these five rode horses that were shod.

"What do you make of it?" Billy inquired.

"A good tracker never jumps to conclusions," Fargo hedged. The logical conclusion was that Utes really were involved and somehow in league with whites. But that was too far-fetched. The Utes had never been particularly friendly. And who could blame them, when, bit by bit, their tribal territory was being whittled away by the never ending influx of settlers and gold seekers?

Many western tribes regarded white expansion as a grave threat, and, in Fargo's opinion, they were right to do so. History proved that. East of the Mississippi, scores of tribes had been either displaced or exterminated. The Utes and others were worried that the same fate awaited them. Yet, to their credit, the Utes had held themselves in check and not gone on the warpath. There had been a few clashes, but nothing serious.

The string of recent attacks might change that. It would only take a mob of hotheaded whites to string up a few innocent Utes and the Rockies would run red with blood. Which gave Fargo added incentive to find those responsible. Not only would he stop the killings, he could prevent an all-out war.

The tracks led higher, always in timber where the killers were less apt to be spotted from afar. They were a smart bunch, these cutthroats. Small wonder no one had been able to catch them yet. Not even the two Arapahos, whose disappearance was a mystery in itself. Fargo was certain they had met with foul play. Otherwise, they would have located the killers by now and reported back to Colonel Tananbaum at Fort Wise.

Up ahead, near the mouth of a canyon, the trees thinned. Fargo drew rein and motioned for Billy to do likewise. "This is as far as you go," he whispered. "Wait here for me."

"Nothing doing. Where you go, I go. How else am I to learn except by watching you do things?"

"Nice try. But you're to listen this time or we're quits." Fargo would only abide so much. If the kid didn't learn to do as he was told, they were going their separate ways.

"All right. I can take a hint. But I've got to tell you, sometimes you're no fun at all."

"Dying is no fun either." Fargo got in the last lick, and cautiously advanced near enough to spot a tendril of smoke rising skyward from deep in the canyon's recesses. He had struck pay dirt. But there might be a lookout.

Concealing the Ovaro in a stand of spruce, Fargo helped himself to the Henry, levered a round into the chamber, and continued on foot. To reach the canyon mouth he had to cross an open area sprinkled with boulders. He scoured it before committing himself, then hunched at the waist and cat-footed to the closest rock. Then on to the next, until he reached a vantage point where he could see into the canyon. Green grass and cottonwoods testified to the presence of water. And where there was water there was bound to be game. An ideal hiding place.

Fargo glanced back to make sure Billy hadn't followed him. The boy was high up a tree, watching, and started to raised a hand to wave but had the presence of mind to lower it and grinned.

"Kids," Fargo muttered as he dashed to the last of the boulders. He was almost in the shadow of the canyon wall, and there was no trace of a lookout. A short sprint brought him through the mouth.

The acrid smell of smoke tingled Fargo's nose. He heard a horse nicker, and the *thuk thuk thuk* of an axe biting into wood. The undergrowth provided enough cover for him to stealthily stalk within a stone's throw of a broad clearing beside a gurgling stream. Picketed to one side in a long string were fourteen horses. Across the way a small fire crackled, and hunkered beside it, about to put coffee on to brew, was a stocky owl hoot whose face was as hard and pitted as the boulders outside the canyon.

A second man had felled a cottonwood and was chopping it up for firewood. He wielded his axe clumsily. Pausing, he mopped his perspiring brow and declared, "Dammit, Stern. I'm sick to death of this waitin' around. When the hell are they going to get here?"

"When it's safe," the man at the fire responded. "The boss is the most careful cuss you'd ever want to meet."

"Maybe so. But I can't take much more of this. I need a drink and I need it bad. Last night I had the shakes for almost an hour."

"That's what you get, Drecker, for polishing off your bottle the first few days we were here." Stern added water to the coffee pot. "You knew as well as I did we might have to stick it out a spell."

Drecker placed his right boot on the cottonwood, angrily swung the axe, and nearly took off his toes. Cursing, he threw the axe to the ground and stomped over to the fire. "Mark my words. If they don't show up by tomorrow night, I'm headin' for Denver and treatin' myself to a night on the town. And don't you try to stop me, neither!"

"I wouldn't dream of it," Stern said. "If you've got a hankering to have your fool head blown off, who am I to stand in your way?"

"You're just tryin' to scare me. But I don't frighten easy."

Stern sat back. "The last man who didn't scare was a fellow by the name of Criswell. He was always giving the boss guff about one thing or another. I reckon he figured the boss was all brains and no guts. But then one night the boss came out to divvy up some money, and while Criswell was counting his greenbacks, the boss walked up behind him, put a shotgun to his noggin, and splattered his brains all over creation." Stern bent over the coffee pot again. "Criswell actually did you a favor by being so stupid. You're his replacement."

Drecker licked his thick lips. "I always took the boss for the kind to hire out his killin'."

"Take four steps back and about three to the right," Stern said.

"Why in hell should I?"

"Humor me."

"I don't see any point to it," Drecker grumbled, but he complied, and when he was standing where Stern had said, he glanced around and snapped, "Well? What do I do now? There's nothin' here."

"There was. One of Criswell's eyes, as I remember. And chunks of his brain."

Like an ungainly grasshopper, Drecker hopped to one side. Stern roared with laughter. They were so preoccupied with their antics, neither noticed Fargo slip from the brush and pad toward them. He hadn't seen any sign of the gold ore but he was confident it had to be there somewhere, and they were going to tell him where, whether they wanted to or not.

Suddenly Drecker looked up and saw him. "What the hell?" he blurted, and stabbed for his hog leg.

6

Some people were born with the brains of a lump of coal. The gunman called Drecker was a living example. Fargo had his Henry trained squarely on Drecker's chest, and, at that range, couldn't possibly miss. Yet Drecker tried to clear leather anyway. All Fargo had to do was twitch his trigger finger to put a hole in the gunny big enough to see through. But he wanted them alive. So as Drecker drew, he rammed the Henry's barrel into the man's gut, and when Drecker doubled over, he brought the stock crashing down on top of the gunman's head.

Stern galvanized to life but he was much too late and much too slow. He nearly went cross-eyed when Fargo gouged the rifle's muzzle into his nose.

"Are you as stupid as your friend?"

"I sure ain't!" Stern exclaimed, flinging both arms into the air. "Whatever you want, you can have. Our horses. Our guns. You name it."

The irony of being branded a bandit by a bandit made Fargo grin. "How about the gold ore you stole?" He tossed Stern's revolver away into the grass.

"I don't have the slightest idea what you're talking about, mister. I wish to God I did have some gold. I'd be off in New Orleans, living it up." Stern wasn't a good liar. Not even halfway close.

"I thought you said you were smarter than your friend." Fargo smashed the Henry against the man's hip.

66

Crying out, Stern clutched his side and toppled onto the ground. He thrashed wildly about, his face a beet, spittle dribbling from the corners of his mouth. He soon subsided and lay noisily sucking air.

"We'll try this again." Fargo shifted so he could slam the rifle against the gunman again if need be. "Keep in mind I can do this all day." He let that sink in. "Where did you hide the ore?"

Stern had learned his lesson. "Up the canyon a piece, in a ravine that branches off to the north. We hid it under a big pile of rocks and dirt. You can't miss it."

"I won't. You and your pard are taking me there."

Stern rose onto a knee, his hands on his hurt hip, his teeth grit against the pain. "I think you broke my hip bone."

"Ask me if I give a damn." Fargo jammed the Henry against the outlaw's chest. "A lot of good people are dead because of you and your friends. They were murdered, then carved up like slaughtered buffalo."

"I'm not the one who did the carving!" Stern replied. "It was some of the others!"

As if that made a difference. Loathing boiled in Fargo like lava in a volcano, and it was all he could do not to shoot the vermin dead then and there. "You're taking me to the ore if you have to crawl the whole way." Stepping back, he poked his boot against the other outlaw a few times, but all Drecker did was groan. "Revive him, and be quick about it."

Hissing like a rattler, Stern managed to bend over his partner and shake him. More groans were the result. "You slugged him so hard he won't come around until this time next year."

"Try again."

It required some doing but eventually Drecker slowly sat up, rubbing his head and stomach, and growled, "You'd better shoot me, mister. If you don't, I swear by the Almighty, before this day is done I'll send you to hell."

"You don't say." Fargo kicked him in the mouth.

Teeth crunched, and scarlet rain spurted from crushed lips. Howling, Drecker flopped around like a fish out of water, his hands over his face. Abruptly propping his blood-smeared hands under him, he lunged at Fargo's throat.

All Fargo had to do was slam the barrel into his gut a second time to deflate him like a ruptured water skin. "Take me to the ravine."

Drecker was a ruin, the front of his shirt stained red, but he made it to his feet with Stern's help, and together they hobbled up the canyon. The looks they cast over their shoulders were poisonous with hate and the promise of swift death if Fargo let down his guard. He stayed well back so he could drop them before they reached him should they prove foolish enough to try anything.

Old tracks showed where the entire gang had gone up the canyon and back again days ago. Six, maybe seven men, all told.

"You could give us a little help, you know," Stern said as the pair negotiated a log with great difficulty.

"I could shoot you both in the foot, too. Then you'd really have something to gripe about." Fargo refused to treat them as other than the brutal, cold-hearted bastards they were. They had shown no mercy to their many victims; they deserved none in return.

The canyon narrowed. Rocky ground replaced the vegetation. At a narrow cleft the outlaws halted.

"The ore is in there about twenty paces," Stern said, nodding, and began to ease onto a flat rock.

"Keep going."

"My hip is killing me. I need to rest."

"You'll have all the rest you need in your grave." Fargo wagged the Henry. They mumbled and swore but they shambled into the ravine to a mound of rocks and earth.

"There. Are you happy now?" Stern was fit to explode.

"Dig out the ore."

Raw resentment fueled their efforts, and within ten minutes they had uncovered a pile of burlap sacks. Stern opened one and out spilled fist-sized pieces of quartz laced rich with gleaming gold. "There are ten sacks, total. Each weighs about fifty pounds. So if you've got any bright ideas about us lugging them out for you, you can chalk me off. The shape my hip is in, I couldn't lift one past my waist."

Drecker said nothing. His lips were swollen to twice their normal size. Whenever he scowled, like now, his shattered teeth were visible.

Fargo wouldn't mind dropping them in their tracks but the army needed to interrogate them. A formal inquiry would be held into the murders, and a public hanging scheduled. He would make it a point to attend. "Back to your camp."

It had to hurt like hell for Drecker to speak but he did so anyway, his speech horribly slurred. "You may think we're licked but you couldn't be more wrong. Our boss is a big man in this territory."

"Shut up, you fool," Stern spat.

"I wasn't fixin' to blab the boss's name, if that's what you're worried about," Drecker said. "I was just settin' this jasper straight. The boss will make him pay for what he's done."

Fargo gave a low whistle to get their attention. "That reminds me. What *is* your boss's handle?"

The pair stopped dead.

"Mister, you can break every bone in my body but you'll never pry it out of me," Stern vowed. "As tough as you are, our boss is ten times worse. So do your worst. You'll just be wasting your time."

Fargo had no doubt he could pry it out of them but it would take a while, and he had no time to spare. All that gold had to be loaded onto pack horses, and then there was the long ride to Denver.

Stern unexpectedly laughed. "When you woke up this morning, mister, did you have any notion it was the last day of your life?"

Intent on the gunmen, Fargo had neglected to watch for other threats. His mistake was borne home when he glanced up and saw four rifles trained on him. Two of those rifles were held by Pierce and Bull Mulligan.

Nearby stood Lute Garner, a big hand wrapped around Billy Arnold's slim neck. "We meet again," he said. "Surprised?"

"Not really." Fargo had suspected the truth when he saw the tracks of those five shod horses. Garner's bunch were like countless others who roamed the frontier relying on their wits and their guns, and who weren't particularly fussy about which side of the law they favored.

"Drop the hardware unless you want your spitting image caught in a crossfire." Garner shook Billy, although not very hard.

Bull Mulligan took a step. "What's gotten into you, Lute? Let's just shoot him and get it over with!"

"We do things my way," Garner responded. "Why must I keep reminding you?"

The odds were too great. Fargo might get three, maybe even four, but certainly not all five. Then there was Billy to consider. He should never have allowed the boy to tag along. He lowered the Henry to the ground. Then, using two fingers, he gingerly lifted the Colt and placed it beside the rifle.

Garner pushed Billy toward Pierce and came over to lay claim to both weapons. He didn't threaten or bluster or do anything other than study Fargo and ask, "Are you a lawman?"

"No."

"Liar!" Bull Mulligan growled. "You've been hovering over us like a hawk for days now. The other night in Denver you sat in on Lute's card game, and then there was that business in the alley. I'll bet you had the kid pick my pockets to try and find evidence against us."

"That could well be," Garner said. "But some things don't add up. He didn't follow us here. He was here when we arrived. How did he know where to come?"

"What *I'd* like to know," Stern interjected, "is what took you and the boys so long? You were due back two days ago."

"We had to fight shy of a band of Arapahos," Garner revealed. "Thirty or more, looking for those other two, I suspect."

Fargo couldn't let the opportunity slip by. "What did you do to the Arapaho scouts the army sent to track you?"

Bull Mulligan laughed. "You expect us to tell you?" Shoving his rifle muzzle against Fargo's ribs, he glanced at Garner. "Say the word and I'll separate him from his innards."

"No."

Mulligan stomped a ponderous foot like a five-year-old throwing a tantrum. "Damn it. Sometimes you confuse the hell out of me. Give me one good reason why I can't buck him out in gore?"

"Because I said so." Garner pushed the barrel aside. "Until I learn who sent him and why, he stays alive. Anyone who gets hasty will answer to me."

Mulligan immediately backed down. "I didn't mean anything, Lute. Honest. We all know how fast you are. You could put a slug between my eyes before I so much as twitch."

"Never forget that." Garner faced Stern and Drecker. "Aren't you two a sight. What did he do? Beat you with a club?"

Drecker gestured at Fargo. "He caught us by surprise, the varmint. Disarmed us, then walloped on us when we couldn't fight back."

Garner gazed past them toward the ravine. "You took

him to where we hid the ore." It was an accusation, not a question.

Stern gestured as if to warn Drecker not to say more but Drecker didn't notice.

"You'd have taken him too if you'd had your mouth stove in." Drecker touched his pulped lower lip. "Look at me! What else were we supposed to do?"

"You should have kept your mouth shut." Garner moved his right hand so it brushed his ivory-handled Remington.

Belatedly, Drecker realized he had blundered. Holding his arms out from his sides, he fearfully exclaimed, "Hold your horses! When I hired on with this outfit, I gave my word to always do as you say. And I've done that."

"I made it clear. If one of us was ever caught, we weren't to say a word," Garner refreshed his memory.

Drecker looked at the others for support but no one met his gaze. Desperate, he grasped at a straw. "I'm not the one you should be mad at! It wasn't me who told about the ravine! I was knocked out cold. When I came to, this fella already knew. So it had to be Stern."

Garner glanced at the other. "Is this true?"

As nervous as a cat on a hot tin roof, Stern nodded. "I thought it would buy us some time so we could turn the tables on him. Figured you would do the same."

"You figured wrong."

Fargo had witnessed a lot of gunplay. Gamblers, assassins, pistoleros, outlaws, shootists of every stripe. He had seen them all. Some were every bit as skilled as they were cracked up to be, so lightning fast, they were a blur when they drew. Few were the equal of Lute Garner. Garner's hand hardly seemed to move, yet the Remington filled his palm, belching lead and smoke.

At the blast Stern staggered back, a hole in the center of his sternum. "There was no call for that," he croaked, and keeled forward, dead on his feet, to smack the dirt with a loud *thud*.

None of the others moved or spoke until Drecker

began shaking his head and mewing, "No, no, no, no, no, no, no!"

As if by magic the Remington reappeared in its holster. "Why don't you go to the stream and wash up?" Lute Garner advised. "We have iodine and other medicine in one of the packs. I'll have Pierce bring it to you."

"You're not going to make wolf bait out of me?"

"Why would I? You did just fine." Garner clapped Drecker on the arm and Drecker nearly jumped out of his skin. "And for the pounding you took, you'll get an extra share. How does two thousand sound? Would you consider that fair?"

Drecker brightened like a newly lit lantern. "Two grand for a few teeth? I'd say that's more than fair." He looked at Garner with newfound devotion, a puppy praised for fetching a stick. "And from here on out, you can count on me for anything. Anything at all. I mean that."

Garner looked down at the still-twitching form of Stern and said a strange thing. "Any excuse to whittle away."

They started back. Guns were pointed at Fargo at all times. Lute Garner walked beside him, hands clasped behind the bear coat, as nonchalant as if they were enjoying a Sunday stroll. Fargo had met few in his wide-flung travels so supremely confident in their own ability.

"These coyotes would like nothing better than to gun you and the boy down," Garner remarked. "So it's best if you play straight with me and don't clam up. Do I make myself clear?"

"As glass," Fargo answered.

"Good. If you're not the law, what brought you here? You didn't just happen by. Was one of those we've killed kin of yours?"

A false answer was on the tip of Fargo's tongue but he bit it off. Garner wasn't to be taken lightly. And Billy's life couldn't be taken seriously enough. "The army hired me. I scout for them from time to time."

"First those two Arapahos. Now you. Army patrols are easy to avoid, but you scouts are another matter."

"Those two Arapahos found you, didn't they?"

"I'm asking the questions. What's your name?"

Fargo told him.

Garner broke stride but resumed walking. "Are you the one they write about in those penny books? The hombre who was in that shooting match in Missouri a while back with the likes of Vin Chadwell, Buck Smith, and Dottie Wheatridge?"

"One and the same," Fargo admitted.

"Well now. Life sure is full of surprises. You're more than half-famous, friend."

"Not by choice. If it wasn't for those writers and their tall tales, no one would know I exist."

"You get talked about in saloons a lot, too," Garner mentioned. "Whenever the talk turns to who's best with a gun. Or who the best tracker is. Or who can scout the best." Garner looked at him. "Your name is near the top of all three lists. I'd call that quite an accomplishment."

Fargo wasn't quite sure what to make of the gunman's compliments. "Life happens," he said, and shrugged.

"You're too modest, Trailsman. But I see your point. Some are lucky enough to be born with a silver spoon in their mouths. The rest of us spend our days dodging piles of cow shit."

Despite the predicament he was in, Fargo smiled.

Thoughtfully bowing his head, the gunman commented, "I've stepped in it big this time around. I'm not making excuses, mind you. But as God is my witness, I never killed any of those people. I take my orders like everyone else."

The revelation stunned Fargo. He had assumed Garner was the leader. "You're not the boss of this outfit?"

Garner made no attempt to lower his voice. "Do you honestly think I would hook up with scum like these if it were up to me? I have to work with them or else."

"Or else what?"

74

A thundercloud formed on the gunman's brow. "We're straying off the path again. Tell me about the kid. Why in hell did you drag him up here? Don't you know any better?"

The vehemence in Garner's tone was like a slap in the face. "He wants to be a scout," Fargo said, realizing even as he said it that it was a sorry excuse for placing Billy's life on the jagged edge of oblivion.

"He must think you're mighty special, how he dresses like you and all," Garner said. "When we caught him, he refused to say where you were even though Bull threatened to blow his head off. Got to admire grit like that."

Fargo tried a heartfelt appeal. "Then let the boy go. He's no real danger to any of you. Make him promise to keep his mouth shut, and send him back to Denver."

"No can do. He's seen us. The boss would throw a fit."

Bull Mulligan had been listening. "Our boss doesn't let us leave witnesses, mister. The dead can't put a noose around our necks, as he likes to say. Women, kids, it doesn't matter. We kill them all."

"Must make you awful proud," Fargo said. But not to Mulligan. He said it to Lute Garner.

A crimson tinge spread from the gunman's neck to his hairline. "You can't judge me without knowing the facts."

Mulligan had more to contribute. "Lute's one mean customer. But he has peculiar notions about killin'. He leaves that little chore for the rest of us."

"The carving up, too." This from Pierce. "He doesn't like to soil his hands with gore."

Something didn't ring true, but Fargo couldn't put his finger on what it was.

In a few moments the clearing spread out before them. Garner ordered Pierce to find the medicine for Drecker and had Bull Mulligan add the Ovaro and the swayback to the string. He personally supervised as the two remaining outlaws placed Fargo and Billy under a tree and bound their wrists and ankles. When they were done, he sent the twosome to rekindle the fire, and hunkered.

"You're a headache I don't need, Fargo. You and this ragamuffin. You're forcing my hand. I don't like that." Plucking a handful of grass out by the roots, Garner scattered it to the wind, unfurled, and moved off into the trees.

"What was that all about?" Billy broke his silence. "We're the ones in a fix, not him."

"There's a chance he's on our side." Fargo shifted to check on the whereabouts of the others. None were looking his way.

"If he is, he has a funny way of showing it." Billy rolled onto his back. "Although he didn't hurt me none when he grabbed me. And when that Mulligan character wanted to backhand me, Garner wouldn't let him."

Turning so he faced the clearing, Fargo bent his legs back until his spurs jabbed his pants. Surreptitiously sliding his hands onto his right leg, near the top of his boot, he tried to pull his pant leg high enough to palm the Arkansas Toothpick. But the rope around his ankles held his pant leg tight to his leg.

"What are you doing that for?" the pint-sized bundle of curiosity asked.

"Say it a little louder, why don't you?" Fargo whispered. "Or maybe you want to stay trussed up like a chicken until they get around to slitting our throats?" His fingers located the Toothpick's smooth hilt but he couldn't budge it.

Without warning, Lute Garner came rushing out of the woods. "Bull! Krist! Mogrom!" he bawled. "Get the pack horses and load up the gold! Pierce, forget about Drecker and lend them a hand. Drecker, stand guard over Fargo and the boy until the rest of us return."

Billy asked the question uppermost on Fargo's own

mind. "What's got him so excited? You'd think the world was coming to an end."

Fargo didn't like it—didn't like it one bit. He scanned the cottonwoods and the heavy undergrowth but saw nothing to account for Garner's behavior. He scanned the high canyon walls, too, but the only sign of life was a raven soaring above them.

"Say, you don't suppose an army patrol is in the area, do you?" Billy hopefully asked.

Fargo doubted it. Colonel Tananbaum was waiting to hear from him before committing to a plan of action. The only other explanation he could think of filled him with unease. Not for his own sake, but for Billy's.

Cradling a rifle in the crook of an elbow, Drecker hurried over. "Give me an excuse to put a bullet into you. Any excuse. Lute said not to kill you but he didn't say we couldn't shoot off a finger or toe."

"Go eat tumbleweed, you polecat!" Billy retorted.

Within twenty minutes Lute Garner and the rest were back, their pack horses laden with sacks of ore. The unshod horses were strung out on a long rope, ready to leave. Only the Ovaro and the swayback were left tethered.

"Why aren't we taking them too?" Bull Mulligan demanded.

Garner had a ready response. "The pinto was seen around Denver. Folks might wonder how we came by it. And the swayback is plumb worthless." He nodded toward the mouth of the canyon. "Head on out. I'll be right behind you."

Wasting no time, the outlaws departed. Lute Garner scoured the canyon wall to the north, then glanced down. "I'm sorry it has to be this way."

"You saw them, didn't you?" Fargo said.

"Just one. Spying on us from up in the rocks. He lit out to fetch the rest." Garner wheeled his sorrel. "If you live, look me up."

Billy coughed a few times from the dust raised by the horses, then said, "I don't understand any of this. Who did he see?"

"One of the Arapahos searching for the two who are missing," Fargo enlightened him. "The whole war party should show up any minute."

"But they'll find us hog-tied and helpless! We'll be slaughtered!"

"That's the general idea."

7

They flitted from tree to tree as silently as spectral wraiths, five swarthy figures clad in buckskins. Four were armed with bows and had arrows notched to buffalo-sinew strings. The fifth held an old single-shot trade rifle, the stock decorated with brass tacks. They reached the tree line and peered across the clearing at the Ovaro and the swayback, then at Skye Fargo and Billy Arnold.

"We're as good as dead!" the boy cried, fiercely twisting his wrists in a vain bid to free himself. "What can we do?"

Fargo was already doing what little he could. He was desperately prying and tugging at the rope around his ankles to loosen it so he could unlimber the Arkansas Toothpick. But the outlaws had done too good a job. It would take hours. Hours he didn't have.

The Arapaho with the rifle threw back his head and yipped like a coyote, an uncanny imitation few could tell was made by human vocal cords. Almost immediately more figures appeared on horseback. Ten. Twenty. Even more. They advanced in a skirmish line, weapons bristling, straight across the clearing, and reined up only a few yards away.

Fargo stopped trying to get at the Toothpick and sat up with his back to the tree. "Don't show any fear," he quietly cautioned. "We might get out of this in one piece yet."

"What makes you say that?"

None of the warriors were wearing war paint. To Fargo that was encouraging. Indians on the warpath generally painted symbols on their horses and shields, and many painted their faces as well. He wished his hands were free so he could use sign language. Smiling, he said one of the few Arapaho words he knew, the equivalent of "pleased to meet you."

An exceptionally tall warrior with the bearing of a leader stared down at them with no hint of friendly greeting. The others were equally cold, equally hostile.

"Do any of you speak the white man's tongue?" Fargo tried in English. A lot of Indians did, if only a smattering. Some had been educated by missionaries or picked it up on their own and were quite fluent. But none of the warriors responded.

Then another rider came up, one who had held back in the trees. Fargo tried not to let his surprise show. It was a woman in a beaded buckskin dress, but what a woman! She was beautiful, truly beautiful, her raven hair luxurious, her lithe body perfect, her face exquisite. Perhaps the most ravishing woman Fargo had ever set eyes on, and that was saying a lot. He greeted her in Arapaho but all she did was stare. Her eyes were lovely, the kind a man could lose himself in for hours.

"What are they fixing to do, do you think?" Billy asked. "Scalp us?"

The tiniest hint of a smile curled the woman's red lips. "Arapahos do not scalp boys," she said in English.

Flabbergasted, Billy declared, "She speaks our language! I didn't know Indians did that."

"There's a lot Indians do that you don't know about," Fargo informed him. To the woman he said, "We'd be obliged if one of you would climb down and cut us loose."

"Why are you tied like this?" The woman's voice was soft, rich, melodious. "Where are the other white men who were here?"

"They spotted your scout and lit out before you arrived." Fargo twisted his wrists as high as he could raise them. "It won't take but a few seconds."

"You have not answered my question." The woman leaned forward, her hands on her mount's neck. "Why did they bind you and leave you behind? They must be your enemies."

Billy's impetuous nature asserted itself. "They sure are, lady! They left us here to be killed, hoping you would finish us off!"

"Let me do the talking," Fargo said harshly. "*All* the talking." He stressed his words so the boy would take the hint.

The woman's eyebrows knit and she said something in Arapaho to the tall warrior. Grunting, he swung down, pulled a long-bladed knife from a sheath on his left hip, and with one slash severed the rope around Fargo's wrists. He gave the ankle rope the same treatment, then turned to Billy.

Rubbing his sore wrists, Fargo slowly rose. Enough arrows were fixed on him to turn him into a pincushion. Extending both hands, backs up, toward the tall warrior, he swept them outward and downward. It was the sign language equivalent of "thank you."

"His name is Big Elk. I am Morning Star," the woman revealed. "We seek my brother, Buffalo Hump, and a friend. They were sent by the bluecoats to find a war party of Utes." She did not try to the hide her anxiety. "They have been gone much too long. I fear for my brother's life."

"We haven't seen your brother. Or any Utes." Fargo saw Billy give him a perplexed look but fortunately the kid kept his mouth shut.

"Is that so?" Morning Star was staring at Billy.

Fargo tapped the boy's shoulder and started backing toward the Ovaro. "If we run into Buffalo Hump we'll be sure to tell him you're searching for him."

All Morning Star had to do was motion to the other

warriors. Half a dozen moved to cut Fargo and Billy off. "I think you speak with two tongues, white man. We will make our fire here a while. You will stay and keep us company."

"You're taking us captive?"

"We would never do that. My people are at peace with the whites." Morning Star grinned. "Consider yourselves our guests, as you whites would say. Whether you want to be or not." She said more to Big Elk in their own tongue, and at his command the warriors climbed down to make camp.

Fargo and Billy were ringed and herded back under the tree. Taking a seat, Fargo selected a blade of grass and stuck the stem between his teeth. "So far, so good," he remarked.

Billy fidgeted like a calf being sized up for slaughter. "You call this good? They're keeping us against our will." He bent closer to whisper. "Why the heck didn't you tell her about the outlaws? She has a right to know they killed her brother."

"And what do you think the Arapahos will do once they find out?" Fargo saw Morning Star and Big Elk casting repeated glances in his direction.

"What else? They'll go tearing out of here after Garner and his gang and wipe them out."

"You're damn right they will. And we don't want that."

"We don't?" Billy shook his head in bewilderment. "But I thought you wanted to put a stop to all the killings. Isn't that why you agreed to help the army? Why not let the Arapahos do the job for you?"

"Garner and that crowd are working for someone else, remember? If the Arapahos massacre them, whoever is pulling their strings will just go out and hire more killers."

Billy nodded. "I get it! You want to keep them alive so they'll lead you to their boss!"

"Not so loud," Fargo whispered. Morning Star and Big

Elk had glanced over again at the boy's outburst. "Just play along with whatever I do."

"You can count on me."

Several Arapahos were gathering wood. Others had gone off in twos and threes, either to explore the canyon or to hunt. Another pair had trotted back toward the canyon mouth. To serve as sentries, Fargo guessed. The Arapahos plainly weren't in any hurry to move on. They were settling in for the night, which was still hours away.

Morning Star walked up and sank onto the grass, her legs primly tucked, her hair cascading over her shoulders. Unlike many Indian women, she wore hers loose, not braided. Idly swiping at a stray wisp, she gazed into Fargo's eyes as if striving to wrest the secrets of his soul. "What is it you are not telling us?"

"I don't know what gave you that notion," Fargo parried.

"You must be one of those whites who believe my people are stupid and inferior. But I assure you we are not. You know something, white man. About my brother, I suspect. About the Utes. And we are not letting you leave until you share your knowledge."

Fargo leaned on an elbow and openly admired her lush body. "It seems to me you're jumping to a lot of conclusions. I've lived among Indians. They're no worse, and no better, than whites. Some are good and decent. Others would stab you in the back as soon as look at you."

"Which am I, would you say?"

"The decent sort. Or you wouldn't bother questioning us. We'd be staked out by now and you'd have us tortured." Fargo gave her both barrels. "You're also one of the finest-looking women it's been my pleasure to meet. A man would give anything for a night with you. Your husband must feel he's the luckiest warrior alive."

"I have no mate," Morning Star said with more than a trace of regret.

"How can that be possible?" Fargo asked. Indian maidens were usually married off young, in some tribes by prearranged unions set up by their parents. "Are the men of your tribe blind?"

Morning Star laughed, then caught herself. "My personal life is not to be discussed. My only interest is my brother, Buffalo Hump. And the Ute war party he and Running Badger were sent to find."

"I'd rather talk about you." Fargo let his gaze dwell on her bosom long enough for her to divine what was on his mind, but not so long she would be insulted. "But if that's the way you want it." He shrugged.

"What are your names?"

Again Fargo went through the introductions. As he did, a shadow fell across them. Unnoticed, Big Elk had come up behind him. Few men, red or white, possessed the skill to do something like that. In sign language he said, "You walk like mountain lion."

The tall warrior folded his powerfully muscled arms across his chest and glared.

"You must excuse him," Morning Star said. "He is Running Badger's cousin. He wants to slice off your fingers one by one until you cooperate but I have convinced him not to." Meaningfully, she added, "For the time being."

Fargo gazed eastward. With each passing moment the outlaws were getting farther and farther away. Not that they could lose him. With all the horses they had, they would leave a trail he could follow in his sleep. But it made more sense to give chase sooner rather than later. So why not meet the Arapahos partway? "I'll be honest with you. Straight tongue. When your brother didn't return, the army hired me to find out what happened to him."

"You expect me to believe this?" Morning Star was skeptical. "Why did you not tell me sooner?"

"Like you, my personal business is my own. And I wasn't sure I could trust you to not go running off after the killers."

Morning Star grasped his wrist. "You can lead us to the Utes? Take us, now! If, as I fear, they have slain Buffalo Hump, they must die."

Fargo placed his hand behind his head and leaned back. She had unwittingly given him the means of gaining the upper hand. "That's exactly why I can't take you."

"I do not understand."

"The army doesn't want the killers wiped out. They want to submit them to the white man's justice. To give them a fair trial and appoint them guests of honor at a necktie social."

"I have lost your path," Morning Star said. "The white man's tongue has too many twists and turns."

"A necktie social is what the whites call a hanging. It's where they take those with bad hearts and string them up by the neck from a rope until they're dead."

Morning Star's eyes widened. "And whites call us savages? These socials. Are they done in private?"

"Sometimes. But in a case like this, with the whole territory in an uproar, they'll make a holiday of it. Everyone for miles around will be invited. The day of the hanging, vendors will sell food and drink to the crowd. Fun and frolic for everyone." Fargo had attended a few public hangings but his taste for them had waned. "You could go if you wanted. Bring your whole tribe."

Morning Star frowned. "I cannot tell when you are serious and when you are not. Whites have proven again and again that they say one thing but mean another. Many of my people believe your kind are born with forked tongues."

"Many of my kind are," Fargo admitted. Two-legged sidewinders were as common as the reptile variety. Maybe more so.

Morning Star, interestingly enough, hadn't removed her hand from his wrist. "So you will not lead us to the Utes? No matter what?"

"I might take one or two of you along," Fargo dangled a carrot before her lovely eyes. "But not the rest. And

I would need your word that the killers will not be harmed except in self-defense."

"You ask much. I love my brother. How can I sit by and do nothing if he has been harmed?"

Big Elk addressed her, and for the next several minutes the two engaged in a heated exchange. Other warriors gathered around to listen.

Fargo had a feeling Big Elk still wanted to stake them out, and that Morning Star was attempting to talk him out of it. He feigned disinterest so as not to worry Billy but when Big Elk abruptly lowered a hand to the hilt of the long-bladed knife, he coiled his legs to spring.

Morning Star went on speaking in a quiet, calm tone. Big Elk gradually relaxed his grip and removed his hand from the knife. Grunting, he headed for the horses.

For a minute Fargo thought the tall warrior was leaving. But Big Elk was only bringing the Ovaro and the swayback over. "Are we going somewhere?"

"We accept your terms," Morning Star said. "Big Elk and I will go with you. We give you our word not to lift a weapon against the Utes unless they threaten our lives." She stood up. "For your sake, I hope you spoke with a straight tongue. Big Elk thinks it is a trick. If so, he will not hesitate to slit your throat."

"What about the rest of your warriors?"

"They will wait here." Morning Star smiled as sweetly as any dove in any saloon Fargo ever visited. "I give you my promise."

Now it was Fargo who was uncertain whether she was serious. She seemed sincere. But women—all women— had a flair for deceiving men when they were of a mind to, and could do it without batting a pretty eyelash. He'd often reflected that men were lucky women had little fondness for poker.

"We can leave now if you are willing." A warrior brought Morning Star's mare over, and gripping its mane, she swung up.

Fargo had an all too brief glimpse of her smooth legs

and a tantalizing hint of rounded thigh, but then Big Elk beckoned him to mount. Being on the Ovaro lent him a renewed sense of confidence. There wasn't a horse anywhere the big stallion couldn't outrun. But he couldn't very well make a break for it. Billy wouldn't be able to keep up. In a race between the swayback and a turtle, the turtle would win.

"Lead the way," Morning Star directed. "We will be right behind you so do not try anything."

"I wouldn't think of it," Fargo bantered. Not with Big Elk bringing up the rear, a bow with a nocked shaft in his hand. Some whites might mistakenly rate the bow as a crude, ineffective weapon, but he knew better. He had seen warriors drop birds on the wing at fifty yards. Witnessed adept archers unleash ten to twenty shafts in the span of a minute. And something told him Big Elk was extremely skilled.

The sentries were on either side of the canyon mouth, behind boulders. They emerged as Fargo approached and let him go by when they saw who he was with. Big Elk spoke quietly to one, who then dashed over to consult with the other.

Fargo had twisted in the saddle and caught their little act. It didn't bode well but he was in no position to do anything. Facing around, he stuck to the trail the outlaws had left. Thanks to all the horses they had, it was as plain as a road. They were traveling northeast, which would eventually bring them to Denver. And to whoever was pulling their strings.

Fargo figured that before too long Morning Star would begin to wonder what he was up to, and she didn't disappoint him. They had been on the go barely ten minutes when she brought her mare up next to the Ovaro.

"My brother and his friend were after Utes. Why do we follow this band of white-eyes?"

"I have my reasons." Fargo refused to reveal the truth until he learned the identity of the sidewinder who masterminded the murders.

"Reasons you are not willing to share with me?"

"I can't. You'll understand why later. Until then you'll just have to trust me." Fargo gave her his most charming smile, but it had no more effect than giving a riled wolverine a pat on the head.

"Your gall is beyond belief, white man. You spin a web of deceit like a spider, then sit there and ask me to take you at your word? Were you to ask the same of Big Elk, he would laugh in your face. Then knock you out of your saddle."

Fargo stuck his chin toward her. "Go ahead. Take a poke if it will make you feel better."

Morning Star started to grin, then adopted a stern expression. "I do not know what to make of you. Part of me thinks you mean to cause us trouble. The other part likes you and thinks maybe I should give you the benefit of the doubt, as I believe whites call it."

"I want the killers brought to bay as much as you do," Fargo assured her. "But it has to be done my way." He devoured her with his eyes. "As far as causing you trouble, there are other things I'd much rather do."

"Are you always so bold with women?" Morning Star frankly demanded.

"A man doesn't get to taste a berry by standing back and admiring the plant it grows on. He has to walk right up and pick it."

Morning Star's full lips quirked. "I sense you are one who has tasted many berries. Your fingers must be tired from so much picking."

"If there's one thing in this world a man can never get tired of, it's berries," Fargo held his own. "The more, the better."

"Some men are content with only one," Morning Star parried. "They live their whole lives tasting only the berry they like most."

"Whites have another expression: to each his own. If a man is happy with one berry, fine. But that's not for me. I like all kinds. Strawberries. Blueberries. Blackberries. A different kind each and every day."

"Each day?" Morning Star tittered. "Are you a bull buffalo, then? With more endurance and strength than ten men?"

"I've never had any complaints."

"The warriors in my tribe would love to hear the secret of how you are able to pick so many. Most do not have your luck."

"Luck has nothing to do with it. Most berries want to be picked. All a man has to do is let them know he's interested, and if they've taken a shine to him, the rest will happen naturally." Fargo looked back at Billy and Big Elk. The boy grinned. The warrior made a show of flexing the string on his bow.

"Perhaps that is how it is among whites," Morning Star was saying. "But among my people it is different. A berry who lets herself be picked too many times is not a berry most warriors would want to share their lodge with. A berry must carefully choose who picks her, and when. And she must be convinced any man who picks her will not let others know she has been picked."

"A lot of berries have that problem," Fargo conceded. "And some men do like to brag about how many they've tasted. But I'm not one of them. Once I've taken my bite, my mouth is shut."

Big Elk called out in Arapaho, and Morning Star raised her reins. "I have enjoyed this talk about berries very much. Maybe we can do it again before we go our separate paths."

"I would like that." Fargo resisted the temptation to turn and smile as she rode back. Big Elk was suspicious enough and might have designs on her himself. Fargo focused on the job at hand. Or tried to. His thoughts kept straying. He could not stop daydreaming about Morning Star. About her exquisite face, exquisite body. About the two of them locked in fiery embrace.

The outlaws had a sizeable lead but the string of un-shod horses was slowing them down. It wasn't more than an hour after leaving the hidden canyon that Fargo spotted a cloud of dust about a mile ahead.

The Arapahos also spotted it, and rode up on either side of him. Big Elk said something, and Morning Star translated. "If these whites do not bring us to the Utes, you will regret it."

"Tell him he must be patient," Fargo instructed her. "A hunter rarely tracks down a bear or a mountain lion in a single day. These things take time."

"He says Utes are not bears or mountain lions. You have until the sun has crossed the sky twice to bring us to them."

"I gave you my word I will lead you to the killers and I meant it," Fargo said.

"Then why are we traveling away from Ute territory instead of toward it?" Morning Star translated. "Ute country is to the southwest."

"Everything will be clear soon enough."

Big Elk growled and Morning Star relayed his sentiments. "It had better be or our people will take out their frustration on you. We do not like being lied to. But whites do it all the time."

The trail curved through some trees. Fargo reined up short of the bend and climbed down. "Wait here." He had gone only a few yards when Morning Star's elbow brushed his arm.

"Big Elk says one of us must be by your side at all times and the other must look after the horses."

"And he chose the horses?"

"I chose you."

The distinction wasn't lost on Fargo. They jogged around the bend to find that the forest ended. Below lay a foothill blanketed in tall, rippling grass that shimmered in the sunlight like burnished strands of copper. To descend while the sun ruled the sky was unwise; the outlaws might be watching their back trail. And to circle around would eat up too much time. "We should wait here until dark," Fargo proposed.

"I think you are right." Morning Star sank onto her knees. "It will give me time to get to know you better." In case he had not gotten the point, she emphasized, "A lot better."

8

One thing about Indian women. When they became interested in a man they generally weren't shy about letting him know. Fargo had no sooner hunkered than Morning Star rested a warm hand on his.

"We have a while before Big Elk comes to see what is taking us. I would like to hear more about you. Where you are from. What you do when you are not working for the bluecoats. Things you like."

"I told you. I like to taste berries." So saying, Fargo pulled her close and glued his mouth to hers. She stiffened in surprise and placed her hands on his chest to push him off but gradually the tension in her voluptuous body drained away. Her fingers lightly scraped the nape of his neck. When he pulled back she was breathing heavily and her cheeks were dark.

"You take too much for granted." Morning Star's right hand fell to her knife. "I have stabbed men for less. Do not do that again unless I say you can."

"You wanted to get to know me." Fargo pulled her close a second time. She had said no but her eyes were saying yes, and her posture, with her back arched and her breasts jutting against her buckskin dress, was as inviting as an engraved invitation. He kissed her. Her lips were soft as melted butter, her tongue liquid satin. When he sucked on it, she moaned deep in her throat and gave a tiny delicious shiver. He drew back and grinned. "Still aim to slit my throat?"

"Maybe later." Morning Star smiled. "You kiss well. Better than any man who has ever kissed me."

"There's more where that came from," Fargo said. But the scrape of a stealthy footstep in the trees behind them nipped his promise in the bud. In the bat of an eye he had taken several strides and was pretending to scan the slopes below. The dust cloud was about where he had seen it last. So were several stick figures on stick horses. He heard Morning Star say a few words in Arapaho, and turned.

Big Elk had emerged.

Fargo knew the warrior had snuck through the woods to spy on them. The question was: How much had Big Elk seen? The Arapaho's expression was hard to read.

Morning Star rose, smiling. Whatever she said to Big Elk elicited no reply. She spoke again, and his answer was slow in coming. She then said something that caused him to whirl and stomp off like a mad moose.

"What was that all about?"

"He wanted to know why I was sitting down. I told him I was resting and he accused me of liking you more than I should." Morning Star smoothed her dress. "He forgets I am a grown woman and can do as I please."

Big Elk wasn't gone long. He returned on horseback and rode by Morning Star without looking at her.

Fargo stepped in front of the warrior's horse. "Where does he think he's going?"

Morning Star posed the question. "He says he is going to get close enough to the whites to count how many there are and see if any Utes are with them."

"Like hell he is." Fargo grabbed the reins to the warrior's mount. "Tell him we should wait until after the sun goes down so—" He got no further.

Bellowing in anger, Big Elk sprang. Fargo tried to side-step, but the tall warrior slammed into him with the impact of a buffalo and bowled him over. Big Elk's shoulder caught him in the breadbasket, whooshing the air from his lungs. He struggled to scramble back up but a moccasin-shod foot clipped him on the chin and sent him sprawling.

Throwing her hands out, Morning Star tried to intervene, but Big Elk brushed her aside and clamped his iron fingers onto Fargo's neck. Too late, Fargo tried to suck in a breath. His air choked off, he grabbed Big Elk's wrists and attempted to tear loose. But the warrior was possessed of the brute strength of a grizzly. Try as he would, Fargo felt himself weakening. He had to do something and he had to do it right then or the Arapaho would strangle him to death.

There was really only one thing *to* do. Fargo smashed a fist where every man was most vulnerable, but nothing happened. His chest fit to burst, Fargo slugged the warrior in the same spot once again, and a third time.

A gurgling grunt escaped Big Elk. Tottering, he protectively covered himself, bending so low, his face was no more than knee-high.

Surging to his feet, Fargo drew back his right boot and delivered a kick that rocked the warrior on his heels. But Big Elk still wouldn't go down. Instead, he drew the long hunting knife at his hip.

Fargo threw his arms up to ward off a thrust. At the very instant Big Elk lunged, a rock as big as an apple smacked against his ear, splitting it and drawing blood. Startled, he forgot about Fargo and spun toward the source.

Billy Arnold had another set to throw. "Leave him be, Indian! He's the only real friend I've got and I'll be hanged if I'll let you kill him!"

Big Elk snarled and started toward the boy but was stopped in midstride by Morning Star, who planted herself in front of him. He tried to shove her out of his way but she clung to his buckskins and railed at him in their tongue. She was mad, and she gave him the sort of tongue-lashing only a woman could give.

The tall warrior hiked a hand as if to slap her, but the fury in her eyes checked his swing. Slowly, almost sheepishly, he lowered it again and bowed his chin like a chastened child.

Fargo lowered his arms. He was sore in spots and his chest hurt but no real harm had been done. It was a reminder, as if any were needed, that he must get his hands on his Colt and the Henry. The sooner, needless to say, the better.

Morning Star was still blistering Big Elk's ears. He answered in monosyllables and grunts. When she pushed him toward his horse, he glumly shambled over to retrieve it. "I am sorry," she said to Fargo. "He has long wanted me. He suspects I like you and he resents it."

Billy dropped the rock. "The fight was over you? And here I thought it was something serious!"

Fargo brushed himself off. The dust cloud was smaller now, the outlaws almost out of sight. "We'll rest here until sundown," he announced, and strode back around the bend to the Ovaro. Leading it into the forest, he sat with his back to a boulder and pulled his hat brim low. Someone came toward him, their tread too light to be Big Elk, their stride too long to be Billy. A foot brushed his leg.

"Are you mad?"

"Hell no. I'm happy as can be. Big Elk tried to kill me. Maybe you should go somewhere else before he tries again."

Morning Star's dress rustled as she eased down beside him. "He has given his word he will not try to harm you again. As stubborn as he can be, he never speaks with two tongues."

Fargo peered at her from under his hat. A stray sunbeam lent her face an angelic glow, and her hair shone like ebony silk. The attack had done nothing to lessen his hunger for her. Quite the opposite. "Where is he now?"

"Where we left him. Keeping watch on the whites down below." Morning Star's smile was as dazzling as a sunrise. "He wants time to himself to think about what he has done."

"And Billy?"

"Your friend said something about brushing his horse." Morning Star pointed at a spot fifty feet away. "It puzzles me. Why does he take such good care of an animal that will soon drop dead?"

"That's the first one he's ever owned." Fargo looked and looked but couldn't spot the youth anywhere.

"I see. I remember my first pony. My mother insisted my father give me one although fathers usually only give them to sons. Mine was black with a white star in the middle of its forehead. I named her Evening Star and thought it so clever because her name was like mine." Morning Star chuckled. "We do such silly things when we are young." She touched his sleeve. "Care to go for a walk?"

"Talk about silly. How will Big Elk take it if he comes looking for you and finds us gone?"

"He knows better than to upset me again. He will not come anywhere near us." Morning Star stretched, her body straining against her dress, accenting her shapely assets. "Of course, if you would rather just talk, that is fine, too."

"Are you sure a rock didn't hit *you* on the head?"

Morning Star grinned. "What is it whites say? I am not one for beating around the bush. When I want something I am not afraid to come right out and say so." Her grin widened. "Does it make you uncomfortable for a woman to want you so much?"

It was loco. Crazy as hell. Insane. Yet Fargo couldn't deny his craving. He glanced toward the bend that hid them from Big Elk. The risk was considerable. Maybe she was right about the warrior wanting to be alone. Then again, maybe Big Elk would change his mind and come looking for her.

"What are you waiting for?" Morning Star teased. "Maybe you do not like to pick berries as much as you led me to believe."

"I'd like to take longer than five minutes."

"Five minutes of pleasure is better than none." Morning Star laughed lightly and playfully traced the outline of his chin. "I guess you are like most men. White or red it makes no difference. Brave in battle but timid under the blankets. How sad we waste this opportunity."

"Waste it, hell." Seizing her wrist, Fargo pulled her into the forest. She giggled as if it were a great game but he didn't share her lighthearted attitude. If Big Elk caught them, the warrior would have no qualms about sticking that hunting knife between his ribs. And he was extremely partial to breathing.

"We should not go too far," Morning Star suggested, "in case they need us."

Fargo disagreed. The farther they went, the less likelihood of the warrior or the boy finding them. He skirted a thicket, plowed through a patch of weeds, and on into a stand of spruce. Halting, he pulled her close, his hands on her superbly rounded bottom. "Just remember. This was your idea."

Morning Star ground against him. "You excite me as few men ever have," she said huskily. "I do not know how or why but you do." Closing her eyes, she tilted her face for a kiss. "Do with me as you will."

Fargo had every intention of doing just that. But rather than kiss her, he knelt and hiked her dress up over her thighs. Smooth and inviting, they were as sheer as silk to his touch.

Morning Star glanced down. "What are you doing? Why are you on your knees? To lick my legs?" She suddenly gasped. "And to lick me *there*! No one has ever done that before. It feels . . . ohhhh!"

At the contact of Fargo's tongue, Morning Star threw back her head and moaned, her fingers hooked in his hair. A few strokes and she quivered and went weak in the legs. He caught her and carefully eased her onto the carpet of pine needles. Spreading her thighs, he knelt and fastened his mouth to her nether knob.

A groan fluttered from Morning Star's throat, followed by a string of Arapaho. She tossed her head from side to side, then bucked upward, locking her heels behind his back. "Ahhhhh. So hot. So very hot."

And so very wet, Fargo noted. It didn't take much more to send her over the precipice. Several strokes of his tongue and she gushed, drenching his mouth with her sweet nectar. Her whole body shook and quaked, and a soft cry escaped her. When the deluge ended she sank back, spent, her breasts heaving, her limbs trembling from the overwhelming intensity of her release.

Fargo slid her dress higher, past the swell of her hips and across her flat abdomen. Her breasts popped free, as full and ripe as fruit, her nipples rigid. Inhaling one, he lathered it with his tongue. Morning Star gave voice to a steady stream of gasps and mews, the whole while her hands were exploring him, caressing him, kneading him. He cupped her other breast and squeezed, and Morning Star bit her lower lip to keep from crying out.

A tiny voice deep in Fargo's mind railed at him that he was asking for trouble. If there was one lesson he had learned, it was to never push his luck. Yet here he was, making love to a maiden not a hundred yards from a warrior who would gladly kill him for daring to do so. It was akin to bating a bear in its den.

Morning Star's hands slid up over his shoulders to the back of his head. She was panting nonstop, her eyelids wanton slits. "You make me so hot, so wet."

Covering both breasts with his hands, Fargo pinched and pulled her nipples. It brought her head up, mouth agape. She fastened it on his and slid her tongue between his teeth. Her fingers tugged urgently at his pants, at his belt. Her inexperience with buckles showed. She couldn't unfasten it and Fargo had to undo it himself. Once he did, she wrenched at his pants as if trying to rip them off. Then, sending a chill of raw delight coursing up his spine, she wrapped a hand around his pole.

A string of words in Arapaho bubbled from Morning Star's cherry lips, words of passion, Fargo guessed. He quivered as she lightly ran her hand up and down his member, her touch as delicate as a feather. He grew warm all over and his breathing became as labored as hers.

"I am ready," Morning Star whispered. "Do it now before the others miss us."

Fargo no longer cared whether they did or not. She had started this. She had enticed him into taking the risk. Now she would see it through. But they would do it his way, not hers. No rushing. No hurry-and-get-it-over-with. He kissed her lips, her cheeks, her ears. He licked her earlobes, her throat. He placed his face between her breasts and ran his tongue around and around each one. Lower down, his right hand was between her legs, caressing, rubbing, massaging. She could not stop trembling. He placed several fingers on her mound and she bit him. Inserting his middle finger, he slid it slowly in until it could go no farther.

A delirium of pure ecstasy gripped her. Morning Star moaned and thrashed. She had forgotten her own advice and was making more noise than was prudent.

Taking hold of her legs, Fargo raised them until her knees were hooked over his shoulders. He rubbed the tip of his manhood along her slick nether lips, then parted them and fed himself into her. Her inner walls enfolded him like a sheath, rippling at the slightest pressure.

Morning Star was the embodiment of female beauty; her head was craned back, her full breasts rising and falling, her hair in glorious disarray. She was every man's dream, the pinnacle of male desire. Most would give anything to be with a woman like her. And would treasure the memory the rest of their days.

Fargo buried his pole to the hilt then held himself

still, relishing the unbelievably stimulating sensation. She wasn't moving either except for the pulsing of a vein in her throat.

"Of the men I have lain with," Morning Star whispered, "you are the best."

Fargo doubted she had been with all that many. Arapahos weren't promiscuous by nature. Like their friends and allies the Cheyenne, they placed a high premium on female chastity. Which further explained why Morning Star was so concerned about being caught. She did not want her reputation sullied. In that respect she was no different from the majority of white women.

At Fargo's first thrust, Morning Star cooed like a dove. At his second, she dug her nails into his shoulders and clung to him as if she were drowning in a whirlpool of pleasure and he was her only means to stay afloat. At his third she groaned louder and longer than ever and fixed wide, unfocused eyes on the cloudless sky.

Fargo set a steady tempo. He constantly roved his hands up and down her hot form, pressing, cupping, stimulating. Gradually, he pumped faster and harder, and she matched him, tit for tat. The feverish slap of their bodies seemed unnaturally loud but that might have been because his nerves were on edge. Try as he would, he couldn't fully relax. Not when Big Elk might come bounding out of the underbrush at any second. He did a hasty scan of their vicinity but saw no one.

Suddenly Morning Star stiffened. She looked at him, her expression unfathomable. One more thrust, and she went wild. She clawed. She bit. She clamped her willowy legs like a vise.

Fargo rode her as he would a bronc. He surged up when she did, dipped when she dipped back down. With a low cry she spurted, drenching his manhood. Her contractions brought on his own release. Although he grit his teeth and tried to hold out a while longer, his body would not be denied.

Of all physical feelings, this was the undisputed best.

Fargo never got enough. Some men couldn't live without whiskey, some couldn't go a day without coffee or sugar or a thousand and one other things. For him it was this. Drifting on a sea of bliss. When for a time the everyday cares of the world receded and pleasure was everything. He could no more do without it than he could do without life.

Coasting to a stop, Fargo lay across Morning Star, totally spent. His breaths were like gusts of wind, his heart hammered. He shut his eyes and was close to dozing off when Morning Star jabbed his side.

"Do you hear that?"

His blood sluggish in his veins, Fargo rose onto an elbow. His ears felt plugged with wax but only momentarily.

"Skye! Skye! Where are you!"

Billy was searching for him! And if the kid kept yelling, Big Elk was bound to investigate. Fargo hastily rose and hitched his pants up. "Wait a while before you show yourself."

Morning Star was pulling herself together. "Are you pleased we did not let the chance slip by?" she asked.

"What do you think?" Fargo rejoined, and kissed her. He heard his name called again. Without delay, he spun and sprinted through the trees until the Ovaro came into sight. Billy was close by, a hand cupped to his mouth.

"Quit your shouting, you dunderhead!"

Billy turned so fast he came within a hair of tripping over his own feet. "Where have you been? I was afraid something had happened to you."

"I was watering the trees."

"You were what?" Billy said, then chortled. "Oh! I get it!" He shoved his hands in his pockets. "Sorry I bothered you. But I couldn't rest and thought you might teach me a few tips about tracking, like you promised."

Fargo had no objections. Anything to take his mind off Morning Star. He brought Billy over to where the earth had been churned by the outlaws and sank onto a knee next to horse droppings. "A scout has to be able to tell how old a trail is." He indicated the droppings. "Break this apart."

Billy's upper lip curled clear to his eyebrows. Or close to it. "You want me to *what*?"

"You can tell how long ago an animal passed by, by how dry their droppings are. Take into account how hot or how cold it's been, and whether it's rained. When it's cool and wet, droppings stay soft longer."

"Isn't there a better way?"

"A tracker has to take a lot more into account than tracks. Now fetch a stick."

Billy's revulsion was transparent but he complied and used it to pry apart the droppings. "It's dry on the outside but not the inside."

"Another couple of hours and it will be dry all the way through," Fargo informed him. "Memorize what it looks like."

"But what about the tracks themselves?" Billy prompted.

"A lot depends on the soil." Fargo scooped out a partial handful of dirt. "Some holds tracks better than others." He motioned to a tree branch waving slightly in the breeze. "Wind is also a factor. It wears tracks down, fills them in with leaves and twigs and dust."

Billy put his palms to his temples. "You're making my head hurt. I never realized there is so much to this. How do you expect me to learn it all?"

"I did." Rising, Fargo patted the boy's shoulder. "Learning a skill takes time. No one ever became an expert tracker overnight."

"But I want to know *now*. I want to be able to get by on my own in a couple of days at the most."

The young were always so impatient, Fargo reflected. It had taken him years to become as good as he was. Years of living off the land. Of learning from experienced frontiersmen and friendly warriors. Years of effort, of hard work. Of never settling for being less than the very best he could be.

Part of Billy's problem was he wanted everything to come easy. He wasn't alone in that regard. A lot of adults had the same outlook. They wanted everything handed to them, if not on a silver platter, then with as little effort as possible. That was not the way of the wild. Struggle was essential to survival if a man was to meet nature on its own terms.

"Don't get me wrong," Billy said. "I'll do whatever it takes. If you want me to play around in horse manure, I'll wallow in the stuff. I'm going to make you proud of me or die trying."

"No need to go to that extreme."

Billy was spared from having to examine more droppings by the arrival of Big Elk. He raked the woods, then asked in sign, "Where is Morning Star?"

"She went off by herself," Fargo fibbed. What the warrior didn't know couldn't hurt him. "She did not say where."

"You should not have let her go alone." Big Elk started barreling toward the trees but stopped when the object of his anxiety appeared.

Morning Star was strolling happily along, humming to herself, a wildflower in her hand. "It is a beautiful day," she said in English, then repeated it in Arapaho.

Big Elk was plainly puzzled by her attitude and Fargo didn't blame him. The maiden wasn't being very discreet. Here she was, on a desperate quest for her missing brother, yet she was acting as if she didn't have a care in the world.

To bring her down from the clouds, Fargo asked, "How long had Buffalo Hump scouted for the army before he disappeared?"

That did the trick. Morning Star stopped humming, gave the flower a final sniff, and cast it aside. "Thank you for reminding me why we are here. My brother was a scout for two winters. He liked the work." She yawned. "I should try to get some rest now. Night will be here soon and I must be ready to ride." She walked toward a grassy spot, Big Elk at her heels.

Fargo tried to sleep but it was a lost cause. Too much was riding on the night's events. Half an hour before the sun was due to sink behind the jagged peaks to the west, he guided the Ovaro out from under the trees. Hardly had he done so than the others joined him. They were as eager as he was.

"What will we do when we catch up to them?" Morning Star inquired as they headed out.

"Spy on them a while," Fargo answered. "So make sure Big Elk keeps those arrows of his on his bow string. There's to be no killing until I say so." He cantered around the bend to the brink of the open slope and reined up to scour the foothills below for sign of the outlaws' campfire. It was well he did. For it wasn't a campfire that caught his eye, but a group of riders approaching from the south. Thirty or better, wearing breechclouts and buckskins, and armed primarily with lances and bows.

They were Utes. Giving voice to a chorus of war whoops, they came on like a pack of rabid wolves.

9

Skye Fargo couldn't say if the Utes were hostile or not. But from the racket they were raising and the weapons they were brandishing, he had no hankering to stick around and find out. He wheeled the Ovaro just as Billy, Morning Star, and Big Elk overtook him.

"We've got trouble! Follow me!"

Fargo went only a dozen yards, then cut into the trees to the north. Outrunning the Utes would take some doing. This was their territory. They knew the lay of the land better than he did. But it wouldn't deter him from trying.

Billy was flapping his legs against the swayback to get it to go faster but it was like trying to wring water from a rock. The two Arapahos were holding back, Big Elk fingering his bow. Fargo reckoned the warrior would as soon stand and fight, as a matter of honor, if nothing else. But honor did a dead man little good, and there were enough Utes to wipe them out without half trying.

Thankfully, the vegetation was thick enough to give the Utes second thoughts about wasting lead and arrows. But there were also a lot of obstacles to be avoided, and that hampered Fargo and his companions. He vaulted a log, ensured the swayback was able to do the same, and faced front just in time to duck under a low limb that came uncomfortably close to taking his head off. For half a mile he held to a gallop, most of it uphill. The Ovaro could go miles more at the same pace, but not so the swayback. The bucket of bones was growing winded. It wouldn't last much longer.

Fargo missed the Henry more than ever. With it, he stood a fair chance of holding the Utes at bay until a parley could be arranged. Unarmed, he might as well throw twigs at them.

"Where are you taking us?" Morning Star shouted.

As if that mattered, Fargo thought. Truth to tell, he was riding by instinct. His sole purpose was to shake the Utes. Where they ended up was nowhere near as important as ending up alive.

A dry wash appeared, the bottom open and flat, and Fargo reined into it to make better time. Five hundred yards farther up was a sawtooth ridge. If they could reach it the Utes would be at a serious disadvantage. The swayback, though, was fading fast. The time it had spent on the trail since leaving Denver was taking its toll.

Fargo glimpsed a snake slithering off under some rocks. A rattler, maybe, since they were common at this elevation. Alert for more, he climbed higher. The slope grew steep, and dirt and stones cascaded from under the stallion's flying hooves. Once he gained the top, he sprang down and over to a boulder at the rim. It wouldn't take much to dislodge it and send it crashing down into their pursuers. But only as a last resort.

The Utes had spread out. A dozen were in the dry wash, about the same number on either side.

Billy pounded up out of the wash and slid off his weary excuse for a horse. "Why did you stop? We can't hold them back if they rush us all at once! We don't have any guns!"

"They don't know that." Fargo took another step and placed his right hand on his holster. To the Utes, who weren't close enough to realize it was empty, it appeared he was going for his six-shooter. They came to a halt.

Seconds later Morning Star and Big Elk gained the

ridge. The latter leaped to the ground and took aim with his powerful bow.

"No!" Fargo yelled, and gestured accordingly in sign language, but the warrior didn't lower it. "Tell him not to let fly!" he shouted to Morning Star. "Or we might as well take our own scalps!"

Morning Star relayed the message and seemed to add a lot on her own. Whatever she said produced the result Fargo wanted, but Big Elk was none too happy. The tall Arapaho turned a resentful countenance toward Fargo and growled several words.

"He says he can drop four or five before they reach us," Morning Star translated.

"What about the other thirty-two?" Fargo shook his head. "There's a better way."

A broad-shouldered Ute handed a lance to another, dismounted, and advanced on foot. His arms were out from his sides to show his intentions were peaceful. He made a perfect target, and Big Elk was quick to take aim.

Fargo took several rapid strides and swatted the bow. For his trouble, the barbed tip was trained on him. Meeting the other's cold gaze, he said to Morning Star, "Remind him the Ute wants to talk. It's in our best interests to hear him out. Maybe we can avoid spilling blood."

"But we *want* to spill blood," Big Elk responded through Morning Star. "They are our enemies. They killed Running Badger and Buffalo Hump."

Fargo's reluctance to tell the pair the truth had put him in a bind. The Utes and Arapahos had never been on the best of terms, and the disappearance of the two scouts was all the more reason for Big Elk to want to see the Utes dead. Fargo glanced at Morning Star. "Advise him again to lower his bow. There is more at stake here than he realizes."

Big Elk was furious but he jerked the bow down. By then the Ute was ten yards below, his keenly intelligent eyes flicking from one to the other. He betrayed no fear, only curiosity. His hands flowed in sign.

"I am Black Hawk of the Mouache."

Fargo had heard of them. The Ute tribe was a loose confederation of seven bands who roamed a vast area stretching from the Great Salt Lake down into the desert country of the Southwest. The Mouache had long held the foothills and eastern range of the Rockies from near Denver south into New Mexico. Despite white inroads, they had made a determined effort to get along peacefully. "We mean your people no harm," he signed.

"Why did you run when you saw us?" Black Hawk asked. "My people have never harmed a white man."

"I did not know what you would do to my friends," Fargo signed, nodding at Morning Star and Big Elk. Calling the tall warrior a friend was a stretch but necessary under the circumstances.

"Arapahos are not welcome in our land," Black Hawk signed. "They are not our brothers. They have killed many Utes."

The Mouache leader was referring to the Battle of Grand Lake, as it was widely known. Many years ago, a combined war party of Arapahos and Cheyenne had attacked a Ute encampment on the lake's shore. The Utes quickly placed their wives and children on rafts and set them adrift for safety's sake, then engaged their enemies in force. After a long, fierce fight that cost many lives on both sides, the Arapahos and Cheyenne were driven off. But the Utes had no cause to celebrate, for during the height of the conflict, freakishily strong winds had churned the surface of the lake into huge waves that capsized the rafts and drowned all the women and children. From that day on, the Utes avoided the lake as bad medicine. And regarded the Arapahos as most bitter enemies.

"Why are Arapahos in Mouache country?" Black Hawk signed.

Morning Star raised her hands to reply but Fargo beat

her to it. "They hunt for two Arapaho scouts sent by the bluecoats. One is the brother of this woman, the other the cousin of this man."

"I know of no scouts. Were they sent to spy on my people?"

"No. In recent moons many whites have been slain and robbed. The scouts were hunting the slayers. As am I."

Black Hawk stood stock still, deep in thought. "These slayers. What will you do when you find them?"

"I will do to them as they have done to so many others. They have bad hearts and must be stopped."

"You will do this even if they are white?"

The manner in which Black Hawk signed the question suggested to Fargo the Ute knew something. "The color of their skin is not important."

"That is good. Because the men you are after have the same skin as you. Three moons ago hunters from my village heard shots and screams. They went close and saw men, white men, chopping up other white men. You might not believe me but I speak with a straight tongue."

Fargo was dumfounded. The attacks started about three months ago. "Your people did nothing? They did not punish the whites? Or go to the wooden lodge of the bluecoats and report it?"

"To kill whites would bring the bluecoats down on us," Black Hawk signed. "So we held a council and debated what to do. Some wanted to send a messenger. Others thought he would not be believed. Most whites do not like us. We see it in their eyes."

Once again the mutual distrust between the two sides had resulted in innocents losing their lives. "Those same whites have killed others since," Fargo signed. "I hope you will not object if my friends and I continue our hunt for them."

"You and your son"—Black Hawk bobbed his head at Billy—"are welcome in our land. The Arapahos must go."

Big Elk bristled like an angry porcupine and began to

raise his bow but stopped at a word from Morning Star. It was rare for a warrior to give in so readily and so often to a woman. Fargo had chalked it up to Big Elk's affection for her, but maybe there was more to it. She had mentioned having other lovers.

Morning Star turned to Black Hawk. "Our peoples have never been brothers. This is true. It is also true we have not made war on one another in more winters than either of us can remember. So I ask you. I beg you. We want only to learn if our loved ones are still alive. Let my friend and me stay in your land for another moon."

Black Hawk was not one for making hasty decisions. Minutes dragged by as he contemplated her request. "I will grant my permission," he signed at last, "if you agree to my conditions."

"We will agree to anything," Morning Star signed.

"You are to leave Mouache land as soon as you find them. If your brother and the other have been killed by the whites, you are not to avenge them. Let the white-eye with you kill them. That way the bluecoats will not bother my people." Black Hawk grew somber. "Heed my words. If you do not, there will be war between Arapaho and Ute, and many will die." Without another sign, he reined around and trotted down to his friends. After a short discussion the entire party headed southwest.

Fargo watched until they were lost from view. That had gone better than he dared hope, all things considered. He swivelled to take up the trail of the outlaws once again, and noticed Morning Star.

Barbs were shooting from her eyes. "You deceived us, Skye Fargo. All this time you knew whites were to blame, didn't you? Yet you let us go on believing it was the Utes."

"I can explain," Fargo offered.

"With more lies?" Morning Star was fit to tear into him. "It is said whites always protect their own. By your acts you prove it true. The whites we have been following are the ones who are to blame, aren't they? Yet you did not tell us. You have been protecting them from us."

Fargo couldn't very well argue the point when it was true. But he had a good reason. All he had to do was make her understand. "If you'll simmer down I'll tell you why."

Morning Star wasn't listening. "Only now, after you have been caught in your lies, do you say you will speak with a straight tongue. But why should we believe you?" She stepped to her mare and climbed on. "We go our separate ways. Do not try to follow us. And do not be surprised if those you have tried so hard to protect soon die anyway."

Fargo didn't like the sound of that. "Are you so mad you're willing to start a war to get back at me? Black Hawk's people will not stand for you killing whites in their country."

"And Arapahos do not stand for their own being rubbed out by *anyone*." With an angry toss of her head, Morning Star trotted westward, Big Elk right beside her.

"Wait!" Fargo called, to no avail. The sun had set, painting the western horizon with bright bands of red that matched his frame of mind. All-out war between the Utes and the Arapahos would reap untold misery. The conflict was bound to spread as the Cheyennes and other tribes were drawn into the conflict. Soon the entire Rocky Mountain region would be aflame with war. And a lot of whites were bound to lose their lives as a consequence.

"Do you always get in this much trouble or did I just happen along when you were on a lucky streak?" Billy Arnold asked.

Fargo had almost forgotten the boy was there. "I do seem to have a knack," he admitted. Which had to be the understatement of the century. But then, life on the frontier was notoriously unpredictable.

"So what now? Do we let the Arapahos kill the outlaws and the Utes kill the Arapahos? Or do we stick our necks out for a bunch of peopie who couldn't care less if we lived or died?''

"The neck-sticking is my department." Fargo had learned his lesson where the boy was concerned. He wasn't putting the boy's life at risk again if he could help it. "Do you think you can find your way back to Denver alone?"

Billy barely hesitated. "Sure. After all you've taught me it should be a cinch." He hitched at his belt. "When do you want me to head out? At first light?"

"Right now." It would free Fargo to deal with the outlaws before the Utes arrived in force.

"But it's almost night." Billy's confidence evaporated like mist under a hot sun. "I've never ridden in the dark before. What if I meet up with a bear or a mountain lion? Do I try to outrun them?"

Fargo couldn't see the swayback outrunning a rabbit. "You need a gun." And there was only one place to get one. "Mount up. We're paying Lute Garner and those curly wolves a visit."

Billy grinned and excitedly slapped his leg. "If I had known being a frontiersman was this much fun, I'd have come west years ago!"

"There's nothing exciting about pushing up mesquite." Fargo took the lead and held to a walk until they were well down the mountain. He gazed to the east and swore. A full moon was rising. It would give them plenty of light to ride by, but it would also give the outlaws light enough to spot them.

The swayback materialized on his left. "What do I do once I reach Denver? You never told me."

"Go to the marshal. Have him send word to Fort Wise. Tell Colonel Tananbaum that I said if he wants to avert a war, he must send a cavalry detachment up here right away. You can guide them."

"Me?" Billy's face practically glowed in the dark. "Do you really think I'm good enough? What if I botch it?"

"You'll do fine. Remember to memorize landmarks on your way down and reverse the order on your way back."

Billy was quiet a while. When he spoke next his voice was laced with emotion. "No one has ever trusted me with anything so important before. I'll lead those troopers, all right, and no one better try to stop us."

Fargo hadn't realized it would mean so much to him. "Just remember. Scouts I teach aren't allowed to get killed. Everyone will think I'm not all I'm cracked up to be."

Billy laughed, then said soberly, "You watch. I'll make you proud of me. As proud as if I were your own son."

They rode the rest of the way in silence over several benighted hills to one that overlooked a grassy basin in which the outlaws had camped. The cutthroats were huddled around their campfire, relaxing. Bull Mulligan and another man were sipping coffee. As Fargo watched, Pierce took a plug of tobacco from his saddlebag and bit off a chaw. Lute Garner sat to one side, aloof.

"I don't see Drecker," Billy whispered.

Neither did Fargo. The horses were picketed to the north, the packs of ore piled near Garner. Krist produced a deck of cards and shuffled them. Mulligan muttered something that made everyone except Lute Garner laugh. When Mulligan reached into a pocket for his money, his vest moved, revealing Fargo's Colt shoved under his waistband. The Henry was beside Pierce.

But where the devil was Drecker? Fargo probed the shadows. One of the animals in the string whinnied, and when he looked, a silhouette was moving along the line, a rifle held negligently. Drecker was serving as sentry. With the Arapahos in the area, Lute Garner was taking every precaution.

Billy had been taking stock of the layout, too. "How are you fixing to get me a weapon? You couldn't get within forty feet without being seen."

The boy had a point. Like most whites, the outlaws had a fire twice as big as it needed to be, although they at least had the good sense to pitch camp in the basin where the flames were less likely to be seen from afar. Sneaking in close enough to snatch a gun without being detected would be next to impossible.

It didn't help that they were under the gun, time-wise, either. Normally, Arapahos didn't do much riding at night. But Morning Star and Big Elk wouldn't be content with waiting until dawn. They would bring the other warriors on fast, and could arrive at any time.

"Stay here," Fargo directed. "I want to take a look around." Swinging to the south, he cautiously crept along the rim until he was close enough to Lute Garner to hit him with a rock.

Garner sat cross-legged, morosely staring into the fire. A mistake on his part, since it would take his eyes a few seconds to adjust if they were attacked and he had to throw lead into the dark.

Just then Drecker ambled over from the string.

"What do you think you're doing?" Garner instantly snapped. "I told you to watch the horses."

"I need some coffee to help me stay awake," Drecker responded. "No harm in grabbin' a quick cup, is there?"

"A quick one," Garner stressed.

Bull Mulligan was examining the cards Pierce had dealt him. "You're frettin' like a mother hen, Lute. We've given those Injuns the slip."

"Even if we haven't," Pierce inserted, "everyone knows Indians don't travel at night. We're safe until morning."

"Go on believing that and your scalps will be hanging from coup sticks before you know it." Garner sat up straighter. "We've lasted this long because we never make mistakes. I'm not about to make one now. My wife and daughter mean too much to me."

Fargo would never have taken the gunman for a family man.

"Before I forget, there's something I've been meanin' to tell you," Bull said. "I had nothin' to do with them, you understand? It was the boss. He came up with the brainstorm. And you know how he is. Once he sets his mind to something, he doesn't like being crossed."

"You've got that right," Pierce commented. "He's buried more jaspers than smallpox."

"Or *had* them buried," Bull amended. "He never gets his own hands dirty when there are others who will do it for the right price."

"He'll get his when the time comes," Lute Garner declared.

"Better not let the boss hear you talk like that," Bull Mulligan advised. "Provokin' him is like provokin' a mad dog."

Pierce looked up. "And don't settle accounts with him just yet, Garner. My poke is nice and fat thanks to this scheme of his. I'd like it a lot fatter before we call it quits."

Fargo kept hoping they would mention their boss by name, but they didn't. He saw Lute Garner give them a look of ill-concealed contempt that did not go unnoticed.

"Listen, mister," Pierce said. "I didn't know you from Adam before I hooked up with this outfit. So I sure as hell don't owe you a damn thing. What's between the boss and you is none of my look out. You'll have to work it out yourselves."

"*If* he ever does." This from an outlaw whose name Fargo hadn't learned yet. "He's not likely to stop until he's rich enough to suit him, and that will take a while."

"Maybe not as long as you think," Bull Mulligan responded. "It's mighty smart of him targetin' only folks who have struck it big. Thanks to his contacts, he knows just who they are. And at the rate we're going, a year from now all of us will be sittin' pretty for the rest of our born days."

Pierce was still staring at Lute Garner. "So it seems to me you should just accept the way things are and make the best of them."

"You're not me," Lute said testily. "It's not your wife and daughter."

"Serves you right for getting hitched," Pierce stated. "A gent like you, with your rep, what were you thinking? That you could buy a house and get a job and live like normal folks? That's a foolish notion if ever I've heard one. A man can't change what he is any more than a polecat can change its stripes."

"Ain't that the truth," Bull agreed. "Sure, I've made some wrong choices along the way. But I've learned to live with 'em. You won't hear me whinin' and moanin'. If I'm turned into maggot bait, well, that's the roll of the dice."

Lute Garner suddenly stood and walked off into the dark to the east.

"He sure is an unsociable cuss," Pierce growled, but only after the gunfighter was out of earshot.

"Mr. High and Mighty, thinking he's so much better than the rest of us," Krist bitterly groused. "Always putting on airs. Always ready to end our days in gunsmoke if we don't kiss his boots."

Bull Mulligan nodded. "I know the boss thinks highly of him and all, but there might come a time, boys, when it's either him or us. I don't blame Garner for being mad. I'd be, too, if I were in his boots. But I'll be damned if I'll let him ruin the good thing we've got going."

"If it comes down to that," Pierce said, "I'd be more than happy to put a slug into his back."

Drecker, having poured himself a cup of coffee, commented, "You sure couldn't do it from the front. None of us could. Hell, even at five to one, he would get most of us before he went down."

"Garner sure is greased lightning with that hog leg," Krist agreed.

Fargo idly glanced toward the horse string and felt a jolt of apprehension ripple down his spine.

A small figure was snaking down the far side of the basin. In the moonlight it was easy to tell who it was. *Billy*. The boy had disobeyed him yet again. And this time it might prove costly.

Drecker cradled his rifle and turned back toward the string.

"Don't forget to wake Pierce up at midnight," Bull Mulligan said. "Krist will take the watch after him."

"What about you?" Drecker asked. "Or are you going to start puttin' on airs like Garner?"

Billy was almost to the horses. He reached for the nearest to cover its muzzle and the bay next to it did exactly what Fargo dreaded one would do. Bobbing its head up and down, it whinnied.

10

Skye Fargo was beginning to wonder if kids *ever* listened to their elders. For the life of him, he couldn't think of what Billy Arnold hoped to accomplish. Unless the boy had recklessly decided to try to get his hands on a weapon himself.

Drecker stopped midway to the string, a tin cup raised to his mouth. He stared at the horses but failed to spot Billy on the other side. Of the four outlaws involved in the card game, only Bull Mulligan looked up. Like Drecker, he didn't spot the boy and went back to playing. As for Lute Garner, he was nowhere to be seen.

Billy had frozen but now he was on the move again, sidling toward the near end of the string. The same end Drecker was strolling toward. Several animals had their ears pricked but so far none of the others had nickered.

Fargo groped for a rock, a stick, anything he could use to save Billy from his own stupidity. His hand came up empty. But he couldn't just lie there and let the boy be killed. Crawling to the right, he ran both hands through the grass, back and forth as wide as he could go. There had to be a rock somewhere. There just had to.

Drecker was only eight or ten yards from the horses, and not more than a dozen from Billy. The boy apparently hadn't spotted him. In another few seconds, Drecker would see him, though.

Fargo's right hand brushed a rock and he scooped it

up. It was about the size of a walnut. Not quite as big as he would like, but it would do. Rising onto his knees, he cocked his arm and let fly. Since Drecker was too far away, he threw it at Pierce but the outlaw bent to pick up a card and the rock sailed over his head and landed smack in the middle of the fire. Which worked out even better. Burning brands and red-hot embers spewed in all directions. Pierce yelped and scrambled backward. Bull Mulligan and Krist shot to their feet, Mulligan swearing lustily. The fourth outlaw was struck by a brand and shrieked like an alley cat.

Drecker whirled, took one look, and raced toward them.

Simultaneously, Fargo cupped a hand to his mouth and imitated the war cry of a Comanche warrior. It had the desired effect. The outlaws dropped their cards and grabbed for their guns. In his haste, Pierce nearly pitched into the fire as he scooped up the Henry.

"Injuns!" Bull Mulligan bawled.

"It must be the Arapahos!" another hollered.

Keeping low, Fargo ran to the left. He had hoped Billy would take advantage of the confusion to get the hell out of there, but the boy had moved to the end of the string and was peering at the outlaws. Any moment, one of them might turn and spy him.

Cupping a hand to his mouth again, Fargo gave voice to another war whoop. Down in the basin Pierce snapped off a shot but he was firing wild.

Billy still hadn't gotten out of there. He was squatting, doing something with the horses.

Damn, Fargo fumed. The boy was going to get himself killed! He began to search for another rock.

"There! I think I see someone!" Krist shouted, and fanned his revolver, spraying lead indiscriminately.

Fargo flattened as hornets buzzed overhead. Footsteps pounded, and when he rose onto his knees, he discovered the outlaws were racing across the basin toward him, Krist reloading on the run. Turning, he bolted westward.

It went against his grain to run but what hope did he have unarmed? Drecker, especially, would love to catch him defenseless and fill him with holes.

Fargo covered fifteen feet. Twenty. The outlaws hadn't reached the top of the basin yet but it was only a matter of seconds. Then there were several high-pitched yips, and the thud of hooves, followed by more gunshots. Fearing for the boy's life, Fargo rotated and sped back to help.

More shouts, from the outlaws this time. Horses were spilling up over the sides, fleeing helter-skelter. Above the din rose Bull Mulligan's roar, "Stop them! Do you hear? Stop them or we'll be stranded afoot in hostile country!"

Every last horse was now in full flight. Hard on their hooves rushed the outlaws, raising a racket that only added to the panic of their mounts.

Among them was Pierce, clutching the Henry. He came to the rim near where Fargo was crouched, trying to grab hold of a sorrel.

Dodging another animal about to run him down, Fargo crept toward the killer. He had to get his rifle.

Pierce caught hold of the sorrel's dangling reins with one hand but the horse was giving him a rough time. It kept rearing, threatening to haul him off his feet. In order to keep his grip, he dropped the Henry and grabbed the reins with both hands.

Fargo could see the Henry's brass receiver glinting dully in the moonlight. Another couple of bounds and it was his again. He brought it up to shoot but Pierce had his back to him and he had never shot a defenseless man in his life.

Confusion reigned. Horses were milling about all over the place. Bull Mulligan had stopped a few. Krist and the fourth gunman were frantically trying to stop others.

Fargo gazed past Pierce into the hollow. Billy had vanished. Hopefully, he had made it out in one piece. Fargo tucked the Henry to his shoulder, about to command the outlaws to throw up their hands. But he never uttered it. A hard object gouged into the base of his neck and a steely warning was whispered in his ear.

"Don't even think it, hombre."

An arm covered in a bearskin sleeve reached in front of Fargo and relieved him of his rifle. Annoyed with himself for being caught flat-footed, Fargo responded, "What now, Garner? A bullet in the brain? Or do I become your prisoner again?"

"Neither."

Fingers tugged at Fargo's shirt and he was hustled into the darkness. When they had gone the better part of thirty yards, the gunman asked, "Where's your pinto and that nag?"

Fargo pointed.

"Head that way. And behave or you'll make me regret my good deed. I'd rather not kill you if I can help it."

"Is that why you left the boy and me for the Arapahos to kill? So it wouldn't be on your own conscience?"

"Give me more credit. The Arapahos aren't on the warpath. They had no cause to harm you. And I was right or you wouldn't be here."

"You took a gamble."

"Life is a gamble. You would have been in more danger if I'd brought you with us. Drecker and Mulligan wanted to gut you like a fish. By leaving you and the kid behind, I did you a favor."

There was a certain logic to the gunman's argument but Fargo still wasn't convinced. "All along you've had our best interests at heart? Is that what you're telling me?"

"I wouldn't expect you to understand. But you're smart enough to know things aren't always as they seem."

The Ovaro and the swayback were right where Fargo had left them. Beside them, fidgeting anxiously, was Billy. "There you are! Did you see what I did?" The boy hurried to meet him, unaware of the gunman an arm's-length behind. "I got to thinking how I could help. How I could keep them busy so you could get your hands on some guns. Did it work?"

Lute Garner stepped into the open, his Remington leveled. "It worked right dandy, runt. Your pard got his hands on his rifle."

"You!" Billy drew up short.

On the far side of the basin the outlaws were still collecting horses. A lot of shouting was going on, Bull Mulligan bellowing like an army sergeant.

"Listen to those jackasses," Garner growled. "Every Indian within twenty miles will know right where we are."

"The Arapahos already do. They'll be here before you know it. If you'll agree to let the boy go, I'll side with you against them."

"Just the kid, huh? Mighty noble of you." Unexpectedly, Garner tossed the Henry to Fargo but kept him covered with the Remington. "Light a shuck, the both of you. Enough people have died as it is."

Fargo looked at the Henry, then at the gunman. "I don't savvy you at all."

"I told you that you wouldn't understand." Garner began to back away. "Let's just say a man can get in too deep through no fault of his own."

Recalling certain comments the outlaws had made, Fargo asked, "Does this have anything to do with your wife and daughter?"

Garner stopped. "How do you know about Elizabeth and Mary?"

"I overheard you and the others talking. Where's your family now? What do they have to do with all this?"

"Everything." Lute Garner bowed his head. His features clouded by shadow, he said quietly, "I love them, Fargo. Love them heart and soul. They mean more to me than anything in creation. And I'll do whatever it takes to keep them from being harmed."

Fargo did some fast thinking. "You were forced into this, weren't you? You have to cooperate or else?"

The reply was barely audible. "Yes." Garner took a deep breath. "Up until a year and a half ago I rode the owl hoot trail down New Mexico way. I robbed banks. I stuck up stages. But I never murdered anyone. I wasn't a killer. Not that way, anyhow."

"What other ways are there?" Billy goaded when the gunman fell silent.

"Gunfights. I've been in more than my share, boy. And the more gunfights a man is in, the more his reputation grows. Soon every punk with an itchy trigger finger is out to get you. Ask Fargo. He can tell you how it is." Garner paused. "Looking back, I can't say I'm proud of what I did. I'd probably still be a hellion if it wasn't for Elizabeth. I met her by chance at a way station. I was fixing to rob the stage she was on, but one look at her and I couldn't. One look into her eyes and I'd do anything to please her."

Fargo believed him. Love sometimes worked wonders, turning even the worst of men good.

"The wonder of it was," Garner said in subdued awe, "that she felt the same way about me. I never figured I was worthy of a decent woman's love but she proved me wrong. For her sake I gave up being an outlaw, gave up spending my nights in saloons, gave up being the man I was. We married and decided to move, to start over somewhere else, a place where no one ever heard of me. That's why we came to Denver."

"But you couldn't escape your past."

Garner's gun hand drooped. "Things were fine for a while. I stored away my six-gun. Traded it for a clerk's apron, if you can believe that. And six months ago Elizabeth gave birth to our daughter, Mary." Garner smiled at the recollection but it instantly changed to a scowl. "A couple of months later it all went to hell. Someone had recognized me. Someone from New Mexico who also came to Denver to start over. Only he had no intention of going straight."

"He's the one behind the murders, isn't he?" Fargo watched Bull Mulligan lead more horses into the basin.

"It's all his idea. He wants to get rich quick, so he has us ambushing pilgrims who strike it rich in the gold fields."

Billy scratched his head. "But you had gone straight. Why did you go back to your old ways?"

"Haven't you been listening?" Garner snapped. "He needed someone to ride herd over his new gang. Someone he could trust not to cheat him. He chose me."

"You could have said no," Billy suggested.

"Do I have to spell it out for you, boy? He threatened to have my wife and daughter killed if I don't do exactly as he wants."

Billy was horrified. "He'd harm a baby? You should have shot him down on the spot!"

Garner's features softened. "I almost did. Until he told me he has men watching Elizabeth and Mary twenty-four hours a day. Insurance, he calls it. If I so much as lift a finger against him, I lose the two people I love most. I'm backed into a corner with no way out."

"Maybe not," Fargo said. "I can help. The assassins don't know me. I can get close to them where you can't."

"I'm obliged for the offer. I truly am. But I have no idea who the bastards are or where to find them."

"Then give me the name of the mastermind."

"Sorry. I can't. If you go nosing around it could get Elizabeth and Mary killed. I have to bide my time and play this out my way."

"While the buzzards you're with go on murdering innocent people?" Fargo shook his head. "Too many have died already. How many more before it stops?" He took a step. "Tell me who is behind it. I'll do my best to keep your family safe."

"No!" Garner jerked the Remington up. "Stay out of this! I mean it. You don't know him like I do. Any whiff of someone nosing around and I lose my family. I won't allow that." He turned partway. "Now get the hell out of here. And don't let me see your faces again." Off he strode.

Fargo moved to the Ovaro, shoved the Henry in the saddle scabbard, and gripped the saddle horn.

"That's it?" Billy said. "We're just riding off? You've got your rifle back. Why don't we *do* something?"

"We are. We're heading for Denver." Fargo swung up. "The only way to stop the killings is to find out who is behind them. And the only way Lute Garner will tell us who it is will be if his wife and daughter are safe."

"Denver is a big town." Billy swung onto the swayback. "Finding them could take forever."

"That's where you're wrong." Fargo had an inspiration. There weren't all that many babies in Denver, and even fewer stores that catered to their needs. "It shouldn't take much time at all."

"If you say so." Billy didn't sound convinced. "But what about the Arapahos? They'll show up here by morning."

"Garner and the others will be long gone. Our only concern now is the mother and her daughter." Fargo clucked to the Ovaro. "Are you up to a long, hard ride?"

"Try me. I can stay awake as long as you can."

Fargo's main worry was the swayback, not Billy. The old horse had lasted longer than he thought it would. Maybe it would surprise him again. He couldn't coddle it, though. Time was crucial. If they rode all night and most of the day, they could reach Denver by late afternoon.

Hour after hour they pressed on, Billy never once complaining. After all they had been through he had to be tired and hungry, but he didn't let it show. The kid had grit, that was for sure. He just might make a fine scout one day.

The night was cool, the sky clear. The moonlight permitted them to hold to a pace they would not have been able to otherwise. Fargo stopped every couple of hours to briefly rest the horses. The only incident occurred at about four in the morning as they were passing through heavy woodland. A snort issued from a thicket to their left and a gigantic form heaved up onto two legs, sniffing loudly.

"Grizzly," Fargo warned, reining up. "Don't move and keep quiet." The bear was only twenty feet away, and he swore its fetid breath fanned his face.

"Wouldn't it be better to ride like hell?" Billy whispered. "Bears can't outrun horses, can they?"

"Yes." Fargo had witnessed it himself on several occasions. Most people equated size with sloth and thought grizzlies were too massive to run very fast, but they couldn't be more wrong. When a griz got up a full head of steam, it could bring down anything on four legs with the exception of antelope, and only when antelope had an edge on flat, open ground.

Still sniffing, the brute took a lumbering step, its formidable front claws raised to rip and rend. A single blow from one of its enormous paws could crush a horse's neck like a brittle twig.

The Ovaro was accustomed to encountering bears, and was wary but not frightened. The swayback, however, was near to panic, and did what most horses would do with a grizzly that close. It snorted and pranced, anxious to get out of there.

"There, there, boy." Billy tried to calm it, patting its neck. "Hold still now. Be brave for me."

The grizzly lumbered closer. From its fearsome maw rumbled an ominous growl.

"It's fixing to charge!" Billy exclaimed.

No, it wasn't, but now it just might. Fargo lowered his right hand to the Henry, prepared to buy the boy time to escape at the potential cost of his own hide. The bear dropped onto all fours, and Fargo braced for a rush. But bears were nothing if not unpredictable, and this one was typical of the breed. With another loud snort, it wheeled and faded into the forest, making no more noise than the wind.

Billy let out a fluttery breath. "Did you see the size of that thing? It could eat a man whole and have room for dessert."

"I've seen grizzlies eat half a buffalo in one meal." Fargo flicked his reins.

The only other wildlife they saw were occasional deer and a raccoon that skittered up a tree and chittered at them like an angry squirrel. Sunrise found them at a stream, the horses guzzling deep. Fargo dipped his face into the invigorating cold water but drank only enough to wet his throat.

Billy had thrown off his hat and was gulping like they had just crossed a desert.

"That's enough," Fargo said, slapping his shoulder. "Drink too much and you'll have a bellyache. Let your horse drink too much and he'll flounder."

They rode on. Since they were making good time Fargo slowed for the swayback's benefit. The temperature climbed swiftly. By noon he was perspiring and famished. And he wasn't the only one.

"Right about now I'd like one of those fancy five-course meals with all the trimmings," Billy remarked. "That, or a raw elk. And don't worry. I'd leave you the hooves and the tail."

"You're mighty generous." Fargo grinned.

By two in the afternoon they had reached the main road west of Denver. Their horses were lathered and weary, but game. Fargo continued to be amazed by the swayback's stamina.

By three the horizon was etched by tall buildings.

By four they were plodding along a dusty street, their animals exhausted. Fargo and Billy were little better off.

Billy could scarcely keep his eyes open. "If I don't get some sleep soon I'm afraid I'll keel over."

The old man at the stable was surprised to see them. He agreed to let them sleep in the tack room, and moments after Billy curled up in a corner he was out to the world. Fargo instructed the stableman to wake him in an hour, and stretched out on his back.

"Only an hour?" the old timer asked. "Are you sure you don't want to sleep a bit longer, sonny? I've seen corpses livelier than you."

"One hour," Fargo reiterated, and closed his eyes. It seemed as if he had been asleep only five or six seconds when he felt a hand on his shoulder, shaking him.

"Mister? Mister? I've been trying for ten minutes now. If you don't wake up soon, I'm letting you sleep."

Fighting for consciousness, Fargo slowly sat up. He had to force his lips to move. "Bucket."

"I didn't quite catch that, sonny. Did you just cuss at me?"

"Throw a bucket of water on me," Fargo directed.

The old man cackled. "You know, you're about the craziest mother's son I've ever met. But if you want to take a bath with your clothes on, who am I to object?" Chortling, he trundled off.

Fargo sank back down. He was so tired, so godawful tired. But he had to get up. In another hour most of the stores would close. He got his elbows under him and made it a few inches off the straw, but that was all. He had no energy, no energy whatsoever. "Damn." He relaxed, closing his eyes, and started to drift off. That was when the water hit him full in the face. A lot of it got into his mouth and his nose, and he came up sputtering.

"Need more?" the old man asked, wagging the up-ended bucket.

"That should do it." Fargo made it to his knees, braced a hand against the wall, and heaved erect. He swayed a bit, then steadied himself. "You wouldn't happen to have any coffee handy, would you?"

"As a matter of fact, I brewed some Borden's earlier and have half a pot left. Follow me to my room at the back."

A rickety chair, a weathered table, and a cot in need

of repair were the liveryman's only creature comforts. And a stove small enough for chipmunks to use. The old man tapped a finger against a coffee pot, announced, "Still warm!," and filled a tin cup that had more dents and dings than a tin roof after a hailstorm. "Here you go."

If Fargo ever made a list of the worst coffee he ever tasted, this would be at the top. It was strong, though. Strong enough to float a horseshoe, and it slammed into his stomach with the impact of an avalanche. His heart pounded and his brain seemed to leap out of his skull.

"You look better already, sonny."

Fargo felt like hell. He gulped a second cup, thanked his benefactor, and by the time he reached the stable doors, he felt alive enough to function. He didn't wake Billy. The boy was a regular trooper but he had already pushed himself to his limit and then some.

The nearest general store was four blocks south. A matronly woman behind the counter eyed him quizzically. "May I help you?"

"Do you sell baby things here?"

"Things?" She made it sound like a foreign word. "Can't you be more specific? What exactly are you in need of?"

"Nursing bottles and rattles and the like."

"We have one of the best selections in Denver. The very latest merchandise." As she talked, the matron moved down the counter and over to a display on a wall. "This, for instance, is the latest rage. Women can't praise them enough." She held out a small object for him to see.

To Fargo it looked for all the world like an imitation nipple. "Why is it so special?"

"It's a new style pacifier. Buy this for your wife and she won't thank you enough." The matron gave him a sly wink.

"I'm not married," Fargo said, and received a glare that could bore through solid stone. "I'm searching for a friend. Elizabeth Garner. She has a six-month-old daughter named Mary. Has she been in after things her baby might need?"

"Can't say as I've ever met the lady, no. Sorry."

Fargo received the same answer from the next three stores he visited. It was pushing six when he entered the Folsom Street Mercantile and Feed Store.

"Why, indeed, I do know her, sir," a middle-aged man wearing spectacles informed him. "A sweet young lady. She left here not two minutes ago, heading south on Folsom. If you hurry you can catch her."

In a heartbeat Fargo was out the door.

11

Fargo caught himself before he made a serious mistake. As much as he wanted to, he couldn't run. It would draw attention. He had to content himself with walking briskly and rising onto his toes every now and then to scour the street. A steady stream of pedestrians flowed in both directions, cramming the boardwalks. Riders, buckboards, wagons, and an occasional carriage flowed to and fro.

Spotting Elizabeth Garner wouldn't be easy. A lot of women were abroad, many toting packages that, from a distance, could be mistaken for little bundles of joy. To add to the problem, the lengthening shadows played tricks with the eyes.

Fargo had gone six blocks when he suddenly came on a woman with a baby. She was admiring the dresses in a shop window. Since it was considered rude for men to accost women in public, he doffed his hat and said politely, "Pardon me, ma'am. You wouldn't happen to be Elizabeth Garner, by any chance, would you?"

"I sure wouldn't," the woman said a trifle coldly, and holding her baby closer, she hurried off.

Jamming his hat back on, Fargo continued his search. It was a long shot, he knew. Elizabeth might have taken a side street. Or stepped into a store. He covered another half-dozen blocks and paused on a corner, debating whether to go back and ask the store clerk if he knew where she lived. Not a second later, a young woman with a baby swaddled in pink stepped from a millinery across the street. Brunette curls framed attractive features. But oddly, for one so young and pretty, a mantle of sadness clung to her like a shroud. Turning, she trudged up Cherry Street, her posture that of a woman with the weight of the world on her shoulders.

Fargo started to cross but stopped with one boot on the boardwalk.

Two unsavory characters lounging in front of a hardware store had straightened when the woman appeared and were now trailing her. There could be no mistake. Their intent expressions marked them as predators on the prowl.

Fargo let them gain half a block before he quickly threaded through the traffic and followed. They never checked behind them. They had no reason to. Secure in the belief no one knew what they were up to, they focused on the pretty young mother. Which worked to Fargo's benefit.

After a few blocks the woman turned left. A quarter of a mile on she turned right, onto a quiet street bordered by quaint homes with small yards, flower beds, and picket fences.

The hard cases hung back, avoiding notice. In a respectable neighborhood they stood out like wolves in a sheep pen. They watched the woman go into a house. No sooner had the door closed behind her than they turned and started back the way they had come.

It caught Fargo off guard. He was only a block behind them. Wheeling left down the nearest side street, he strolled purposefully up a short path to a porch flanked by a trellis. From behind it he saw the pair cross the intersection and proceed toward the heart of town. He turned to shadow them and heard the front door latch rasp.

"What do you think you're doing?" a portly middle-aged woman demanded. In her pudgy fist she held a olled-up newspaper. "This is private property. Riffraff re not welcome. Go away or I'll swat you."

Fargo nodded at the trellis. "I was just admiring your oses, ma'am." He got out of there before she made ood on her threat and swiftly overtook his quarry. The air sauntered along as if they owned the boardwalk, humbs hooked in their gunbelts. One was rake thin with reasy black hair. The other looked as if no one ever old him water was good for something besides drinking.

Hoping they would lead him to their boss, Fargo followed them west to a seamy section of Denver notorious or its rowdy element and wild night life. They entered he Bull's Head Saloon. Classier than most saloons, its oker tables were covered in felt, the drinks were served n a mahogany bar, and the piano player actually knew ow to play. Greasy and Grimy, as Fargo had nicknamed hem, picked a corner table and sat down with their acks to the wall. They ordered beers. Every so often ne or the other glanced at the entrance, a sure sign they vere waiting for someone.

At the far end of the bar, where he could watch them innoticed, Fargo nursed a whiskey. Each time the door pened he looked up. But it was never the expected hird party. Greasy pulled a pocket watch from his vest, onsulted it, and made a comment that caused Grimy o frown.

An hour had gone by when a beefy gunman barreled n, surveyed the tables, and angled straight toward theirs. They greeted him warmly, and Fargo thought he heard Greasy call the newcomer Harve. The trio huddled, their heads over the table, and whatever news Harve brought lid not go over well.

Half an hour crawled by. It became obvious they veren't going anywhere anytime soon, and equally obvi- us they weren't expecting anyone else. Fargo had waited ong enough. Downing the last of his drink, he bent his steps to the house on Fremont, again removed his hat, nd knocked lightly on the door.

Although the sun had yet to set, lamps were lit inside and a shadow moved across a window to his right. Fingers parted a curtain and a voice tinged with apprehension asked, "Who are you and what do you want?"

"Are you Mrs. Garner?"

"Who wants to know?" she suspiciously demanded.

"Someone who would like to help Lute and you."

The curtain was jerked shut. Inside, a bolt was thrown and the door opened wide enough to reveal the twin muzzles of a double-barreled shotgun. "Help us how?"

Fargo noticed the twin hammers were cocked and her finger was curled around the triggers. One twitch and she would blow his head clean off. "I know about the bind your husband is in. About the men who are watching you. And what they'll do if your husband doesn't go along with what they want."

"You're a friend of his? Who are you? How is it I've never set eyes on you before?"

Fargo introduced himself. "The army hired me. I'd like to stop the killing, but I can't until I learn who is behind it. Your husband won't tell me so long as you're in danger, so—"

"So you hunted me down to save me?" Elizabeth broke in. "But all you've done is made things worse. They'll see you!"

"The two men who were watching you are at a saloon." Fargo thought that would calm her but she took a step and jammed the shotgun against his chest.

"What about the other two?"

A knot formed deep in Fargo's gut. "Other two?" he repeated.

"Two follow me about during the day. Two others keep watch over the house at night. They think I don't know. But I couldn't help but spot them after all these weeks." Elizabeth glanced up and down the street. "If they see you—" Suddenly she gasped, skipped back inside, and slammed the door.

Fargo heard heavy footsteps coming down the walk.

He wanted to kick himself. It had never occurred to him he gunnies might work in shifts. The new pair had been concealed at the far end of the block, rough customers like those in the saloon. They pushed open the gate.

"Who the hell are you, mister? And what are you doing here?" The speaker was a cocky runt with a Smith and Wesson strapped to his waist.

"I don't see that's any of your business," Fargo replied. Common sense told him to avoid gunplay. But he was tired, sore, and hungry, and most of all, he was fed up with being pushed around.

"That's where you're wrong," the same gunman informed him. "This lady is under our protection, you might say. Anyone who pays her a visit has to tell us who they are and why they're here. So start flapping your gums."

"You took the words right out of my mouth." Fargo had reached the end of his tether. "Tell me who you work for and you might live out the day."

The men swapped glances and the talkative one said, "Mister, your ears must be plugged with wax. You've got this all backwards. Throw down that rifle. You're coming with us."

"That'll be the day," Fargo said dryly.

Their hands swooped to their six-guns and they were clearing leather when Fargo blasted a shot from the hip, worked the Henry's lever, and sent a second slug into the other gunman. Both staggered but only the second man fell. The runt caught hold of the picket fence and tried to take a deliberate bead. A round between the eyes dissuaded him.

The front door opened again, framing Elizabeth Garber. She had the shotgun in one hand, the baby in her other arm. "What have you done?" she blurted. "They'll think Lute put you up to this!"

"Then we have to get you out of here." Gripping her wrist, Fargo pulled her toward the gate but she dug in her heels.

"We can't! You don't understand!"

Doors were opening up and down the street. Shou[ts]
broke out. Someone might think to send for the law.

Fargo placed a hand on her shoulder. "Listen to m[e.]
Lute won't be harmed if I reach him first. And I kno[w]
right where to find him. We'll hide you somewhere unt[il]
this blows over and—"

Again Elizabeth cut him off. "Like blue blazes yo[u]
will! You're taking me to him, and I won't brook a[ny]
argument." She shoved the shotgun at him. "Hold on [to]
this. I need to collect things for the baby."

A few doors down a man bellowed, "What's going o[n]
over there, Mrs. Garner? Are you all right?"

"I'm fine, Mr. Lewis!" Elizabeth spun. To Fargo sh[e]
whispered, "Meet me out back in two minutes." The[n]
she darted indoors.

Shouts from far off warned Fargo news of the gun[-]
fight was spreading like a prairie fire. Before long
hordes of curious citizens would throng to the scene[.]
Bloodletting always attracted crowds like dead mea[t]
attracted flies.

Fargo ran around to the rear. He was concerned abou[t]
the three gunmen. They were bound to hear of it. When[-]
ever there was gunplay, some busybody or other took [it]
on themselves to rush from saloon to saloon spreadin[g]
the word.

The screen door creaked and out bustled Elizabet[h]
Garner. She had Mary and a large bag bursting at th[e]
seams with clothes and baby items. "I'm ready. Lea[d]
the way."

A narrow gate opened onto an alley. Fargo opened i[t]
for her and steered her away from the center of town[.]
It was best to swing wide and avoid the gathering throng[.]
"About you going with me to see Lute—"

"I am, and that's final." Elizabeth indulged her habi[t]
for interrupting. "This has to end, one way or the other[.]
I am sick to death of being allowed to see him only [a]

few hours every couple of weeks. If you know where he is, you're taking me to him."

"He's up in the mountains. It'll take two to three days to reach him with the baby along. Only one day if I go by myself."

"You're saying that it's in Lute's best interests for me not to go? You're saying I'm being selfish?" Elizabeth's lips pinched together. "Do you have any idea how much I miss him? Of the nightmare I've been through, never knowing from one day to the next if he was still alive?"

"He won't be for long if I don't get to him in time," Fargo stressed. For the longest while she was quiet. As they neared the stable he related his plan.

"I suppose your way is best," Elizabeth said. "With the baby and me safe, Lute will be free to end this. But you be sure to tell him I wanted to go with you. Be sure to tell him how much I love him."

"I will," Fargo promised.

Waking Billy was a chore. The youth was sawing petrified logs. Fargo had to shake him a dozen times before he stirred, and even then Billy merely cracked an eyelid and mumbled, "Let me be. I don't want to be woke up until Christmas."

"You have a job to do." Fargo beckoned Elizabeth over. "I'm trusting you to escort Mrs. Garner and her baby to Fort Wise. You need to start right away."

Billy struggled up. "Pleased to meet you, ma'am." He yawned, then shook himself. "We're to travel at night? Just the three of us? Where will you be?"

"I'm heading back up into the high country." Fargo placed the shotgun beside him. "Always keep this handy. It can blow a hole as big as a watermelon in man or beast."

The stableman was all too glad to rent a horse to Elizabeth. He fussed over her as if she were a princess and insisted on picking out the gentlest animal he had. "No rush on returning it, ma'am. Take an extra day or two if you want and I won't charge you."

"You old goat," Fargo said out the corner of his mouth as they rode through the double doors, and the old man cackled.

Night had fallen. Fargo imagined that by now the outlaw leader had learned about runt and the other gunny and must have every hard case in his employ out scouring the streets for Elizabeth and Mary. Which was why he elected to tag along until they passed the city limits. They came to the end of the block, and he reined right and encountered the last person in the world he expected to meet.

Matt Dirkson was mounted on a fine chestnut. The banker was dressed in a suit and bowler hat, as before, but now he had a gunbelt strapped around his waist. And his saddle was rigged with a bedroll. "Well, look who it is," he said, by way of greeting.

"Out of our way." Fargo had no time to spare for the jealous coyote.

"Think you're going somewhere, do you?" Dirkson smirked, then snapped his fingers.

Riders suddenly came out of the shadows on either side. More came up from behind. Nine in all, including the three gunmen Fargo last saw at the Bull's Head Saloon. With a start he realized Dirkson had been waiting for them, and insight stabbed through him like a knife. "It can't be."

"That's what I said when witnesses described the man who gunned down two of my boys earlier," Dirkson responded. "I knew it was you. And it dawned on me that our run-in at Molly's must have been part of some scheme to ferret out information about me."

Fargo couldn't get over it. The mastermind was the banker! Yet it shouldn't surprise him. Dirkson had his finger on the pulse of the business community. That included news of the latest gold strikes, often before they became common knowledge. And there was no denying the man was ruthless. Now that Fargo thought about it, it made perfect sense. "I didn't know about the murders when we met at Molly's," he said, as much to stall as anything else. Were he alone, he would make a break for it. But not with the infant and mother at his side. To say nothing of Billy.

Dirkson was perplexed. "You didn't? Then why are you helping Lute Garner's woman? Would you have me believe it was coincidence?"

Before Fargo could answer, Elizabeth interjected, "So you're the one who has my husband over a barrel? You're the one who has turned our life into a shambles? I should claw your eyes out!" Had it not been for the baby in her arms, she clearly would have thrown herself at him.

Billy had absorbed the latest development in confused silence. But now he jerked up the shotgun. Or tried to. The gunman Fargo had nicknamed Greasy was a shade faster and ripped it from his grasp.

"Thanks for reminding me, boy," Dirkson said. At a nod from him, Grimy relieved Fargo of the Henry. "Now then. We're all going for a ride up into the mountains. Behave, and you'll live a lot longer."

"You can't get away with kidnaping people in public!" Elizabeth declared.

"I already have," Dirkson scoffed. "Look around you. Do you see anyone paying the least bit of attention to us? No. Why should they? They don't know what's going on, and they don't care."

"I'll scream!" Elizabeth said.

"Go right ahead, my dear," Dirkson said. "But know that the moment you do, my men will shoot your would-be rescuers from their saddles. I'll say they tried to rob me. And if you should take a stray bullet, well, that's just how these things work out sometimes, isn't it?"

"You're scum, Matt Dirkson. Pure and total scum."

"Now, now. Flattery always embarrasses me." Snickering, Dirkson motioned again, and started up the street.

Hemmed by lead throwers, Fargo and his friends had no recourse but to do the same.

Matt Dirkson glanced at him. "In case you're wondering, one of my men spotted you after you left her place and saw you go into the stable. So I had it surrounded."

"Why?" Fargo asked.

"Why else? To keep her from escaping. Her husband performs an invaluable service for me." Dirkson tilted his head. "Oh. That isn't what you meant, is it?"

"You're a banker. You earn good money. Everyone looks up to you as a pillar of the community. Why throw it all away to get rich quick?"

"Is that what you think?" Dirkson snorted. "My ambition is loftier than that. Yes, I'm vice president of a prestigious financial institution. That, and a dollar, will get me a dollar meal. But it's not about the money. The gold is a means to an end, nothing more."

Fargo waited for him to elaborate and Dirkson didn't disappoint him. The man loved to hear the sound of his own voice.

"Look around you. Denver is growing by leaps and bounds. In a few years it will be the biggest city between the Mississippi River and the Pacific Ocean. We'll have our own territorial legislature and governor. After that, statehood."

Fargo still didn't understand, and said so.

"It boils down to opportunity and having the intelligence to seize the chance of a lifetime. It's not wealth I'm after, it's *power*. I intend to become the most powerful man in the territory. The title of governor would suit me nicely. After that, who knows? It could be a springboard to national power. Senator, perhaps. Or even a higher office." Dirkson practically glowed with fervor. "I've always wanted to sit in the White House."

"You're loco."

"On the contrary, Mr. Fargo. I have my rise to prominence planned down to the finest detail. The first step is to acquire more gold than Midas. I'll have a grand estate and be able to afford the best of everything money can buy."

"Fancy trappings won't make you president."

"Ah. But hobnobbing with those in positions of influence will. It's not what you do in this world that counts. It's who you know. The gold I'm stealing will open new doors for me. I'll rub elbows with those who make policy and mold careers. And in the process, mold my own."

"And what about all the people you've had killed?"

"What about them? They're nobodies. Dregs who never amounted to much. They wouldn't use their gold to its best advantage. I will."

"The end justifies the means," Fargo said sarcastically.

"Always. Anyone who thinks otherwise is a fool." Dirkson paused. "Every great venture has its cost. So a few people die to provide the wealth I require. So what? In the greater scheme of things they are insignificant. Gnats to be swatted aside so I might claim my rightful destiny."

"I said it before. You're loco."

"Oh, please. I won't be the first to use the backs of others as my stepping stones to power. It's a cutthroat world in which we live. The greatest rewards go to those who have no qualms about doing whatever is necessary to reach the top. You call that crazy. I call it being practical."

"Call it whatever you want," Fargo snapped. "Killing is just plain wrong."

Dirkson stared at him. "Surely you, of all people, should know better. You're a frontiersman. You know survival goes to the fittest. That's the natural order of things. How can you sit there and look down your nose at me for doing what comes naturally?"

"Sugarcoat it any way you want. But mountain lions don't kill other mountain lions to lord it over the rest."

"Ah. It just so happens I know more about wildlife than you think. I know, for instance, that male mountain lions fight and kill other males over territory and the right to mate with females. In other words, they fight, and kill, for *power*. Exactly the same as I'm doing."

"There's a difference," Fargo argued. "The cats do it because they *have* to. You do it because you *want* to."

"I fail to see the distinction," Dirkson sniffed. "It's moot, anyway. I'll be damned if I'll let petty moral considerations stop me from fulfilling my dream. Or let you or anyone else thwart me."

They had reached Denver's outskirts and were on a narrow road which, in a few blocks, linked up with the rutted track that wound up into the high country.

Fargo shifted in his saddle. Elizabeth was a study in misery, Mary clasped tight to her bosom. He smiled to encourage her but she was too depressed to respond. Billy, on the other hand, held his head high and glared defiantly at their captors, a scrapper if ever there was one. Turning back to Dirkson, Fargo remarked, "There's a flaw in this great plan of yours."

"Nonsense. It's foolproof."

"You're forgetting Bull Mulligan and Pierce and the rest of your gunnies."

"How can they possibly cause a problem? So long as I pay them their cuts, they'll jump over cactus for me."

"For now. But what if one of them becomes greedy? They know how you're going about lining your pockets. They could blackmail you once you're rich and powerful."

"Don't be ridiculous." But the way Dirkson said it, he didn't think the notion was as preposterous as he tried to make it sound.

Fargo shrugged. "All I know is, if it were me, I wouldn't want anyone to hold something like that over my head."

"You talk too much."

For the next several hours hardly a word was spoken. Dirkson insisted on riding hard to reach a certain ridge by midnight. He also refused to allow a fire. Greasy and Grimy bound Fargo and Billy but Elizabeth was spared.

"Only so you can keep your brat quiet," Dirkson informed her. "Sound travels a long way out here at night, and you never know who's listening." He placed a hand on her shoulder. "One other thing. Try sneaking off and your husband's life is forfeit."

"You wouldn't dare!" Elizabeth replied, shrugging the hand off. "You need Lute. You've said so yourself."

"He's a rare one, madam. I'll grant you that. A gunfighter with a sense of honor. Which is why I knew I could trust him to keep a tight rein on the others. But he's not indispensable. I can find a replacement. Keep that in mind if you have any ideas in that pretty head of yours about escaping."

"I hope you rot in hell."

"Now, now. Spite is most unbecoming." Chuckling, Dirkson strolled over to his men.

Elizabeth began gently rocking her baby. "He's planning to murder us like he has all those others, Mr. Fargo. I can feel it in my bones." She tenderly kissed Mary's forehead, tears brimming her eyes. "What are we going to do?"

Fargo wished to hell he knew.

12

Skye Fargo still had his ace in the hole, the Arkansas Toothpick strapped to his right ankle. But he wasn't given the chance to use it. During the day he was surrounded by hawkeyed killers under order from Matt Dirkson to turn him into a sieve if he twitched wrong. At night they bound him, wrists and legs.

Then, late in the afternoon of the third day, Dirkson drew rein on a mountainside overlooking a narrow valley. Below, horses grazed in a grassy meadow and men were moving about under the trees. "They're here! Exactly as they should be."

Fargo had no need to ask who "they" were. As he descended, he spotted Bull Mulligan, Drecker, and Krist hunkered beside a fire.

"We have several rendezvous sites," Dirkson offhandedly mentioned. "I alternate them so no one can catch on to what we're up to."

"You must know the mountains well." Which surprised Fargo. He hadn't taken the banker for the outdoors type.

"Oh, not me. One of my men, Pierce is his name, has been all over these peaks and back again, grubbing for gold. He never found enough to make it worth his while, but he's making good money now working for me. He and I spent a couple of weeks up here about six months ago, scouting for places like this one." Dirkson grinned.

"As I've been telling you, I have this worked out down to the smallest detail."

Elizabeth rose in the stirrups and anxiously scanned the woods. When a tall figure in a bearskin coat emerged, she squealed in delight and tried to goad her mount on ahead but the gunman beside her wouldn't let her by. "Get out of my way, damn you!" she fumed. "I want to go to my husband!"

"Be patient, my dear," Dirkson chided. "Another couple of minutes and your wish will be granted."

Someone caught sight of them and raised a shout. Lute Garner glanced up. Even at that distance Fargo saw the shock of recognition. Lute hastened toward the spot where the trail reached the valley floor and was waiting for them when they got there.

With a grand flourish Matt Dirkson declared, "Mr. Garner! I've brought someone to see you. I trust you won't hold it against me once you've learned the circumstances."

Garner marched past the banker without so much as a glance. A gunman on horseback failed to get out of his way fast enough, and with an incredibly swift lunge, Garner grabbed the man and flung him to the ground. The gunman sat up and made as if to draw but decided against it.

Lute Garner smacked the horse to get it out of his way. And then he was next to Elizabeth's mount, and she slid off into his arms, Mary nestled between them. Elizabeth buried her face in the folds of his bearskin coat, her body trembling, and gave birth to great, racking sobs.

Some of the gunnies grinned and winked at one another. They found the family reunion hilarious. But their grins died when Lute Garner raked them with a stare that would melt ice.

Bull Mulligan arrived. He thrust his hand at the banker. "Great to see you again, Mr. Dirkson. We had a good haul this time."

Pierce was only a few yards away. "It's a wonder we made it here, boss. A band of Arapahos is out for our scalps, and they've been dogging us for days."

"Arapahos?" Dirkson said in alarm, glancing up and down the valley "Where are they now?"

"Don't worry," Bull Mulligan said. "We lost them yesterday morning on some rocky ground south of here. Haven't seen hide nor hair of them since."

Fargo scanned the valley, too. He thought it highly unlikely the outlaws had given a band of seasoned warriors the slip. Big Elk and Morning Star might be biding their time, waiting for the right moment to strike.

"Where did you find these two jaspers?" Mulligan pointed at Fargo and Billy. "Last we knew, we'd left them trussed up like lambs for the slaughter."

"You took them prisoner and they got away? Evidently I have some catching up to do." Dirkson rode toward the campfire. "I hope you have coffee on. I could use some."

Not counting Lute Garner, Fargo tallied fifteen gunmen. Garner took his wife and infant daughter to shelter under a fir tree where they could be by themselves. The rest gathered close, completely surrounding Fargo and Billy.

Matt Dirkson examined the bags of ore, then listened to an account by Bull Mulligan of the attack on the ore wagon, their run-in with Fargo, and the subsequent Arapaho pursuit.

"All in all, it's been a hell of a week," Mulligan concluded. "But the worst is over and we have more gold to divvy up."

"All in good time," Dirkson said between sips of coffee. "You know the routine. First, I'll have the ore appraised, then I'll convert it into currency and bring you your share."

Pierce gleefully rubbed his palms together. "At the rate we're going, I'll soon have enough squirreled away to go on a spree the likes of which will have me soused for a month."

"There's a lot more to life than whiskey and women," Dirkson told him.

"Not where I'm concerned." Pierce was about to add something but he stopped, blinked, and whispered out the side of his mouth, "Don't look now, boss, but I think trouble is coming."

Lute Garner was approaching. He had removed his bearskin coat for the first time since Fargo met him, revealing a blue homespun shirt probably made for him by Elizabeth. His right hand brushed the holster to his ivory-handled Remington. Some of the outlaws noticed and nudged one another.

Dirkson plastered a smile on his devious face. "It's about time you came over to see me, Lute. I was beginning to feel neglected."

Garner nodded at Fargo, and halted. His shoulders were squared, his jaw set. He had the look of a man who had made up his mind about something and was determined to see it through come hell or high water. "You had no call bringing them here."

"I beg to differ," Dirkson glibly responded. "If you must blame someone, blame your friend, Fargo. I was content to keep an eye on them from afar and let them go about their lives. But Mr. Fargo interfered. He killed two of my men and came close to spiriting your wife and daughter away. I couldn't permit that."

Garner looked at Fargo. "I thank you for what you tried to do. But I told you to stay out of this. You should have listened."

Dirkson studied the gunfighter. "So he was doing it on his own? Interesting. I would never have taken him for a do-gooder. I'm compelled to grant a reprieve to you and your family. When I go back down, your wife and daughter go with me. Things will be just as they were."

"No."

The banker's eyebrows met over his nose. "Are you presuming to dictate the terms of our arrangement? Need I remind you how outnumbered you are?"

"I can count." Lute was exceptionally calm given the circumstances. "You made a mistake bringing them here, Dirkson. It's reminded me of how much I care for them. And how wrong I was not to stand up to you from the start."

"What can you hope to accomplish? You might gun me but the rest will drop you where you stand. And where does that leave Elizabeth and Mary? Do you want them left at the mercy of men like Bull and Pierce?"

Pierce snickered and smacked his lips. "I know just how to treat a sweet little gal like her."

Lute Garner's flinty eyes bored into Dirkson's. "I'll gun you, all right. And this scrawny bastard and a lot of others before they take me down. Either that, or you let me take my family out of here right this minute."

Raw rage twisted Matt Dirkson's visage. Bull Mulligan, Pierce, and others were poised to unlimber their hardware. Tension crackled like a lit fuse, and it wouldn't take much for the powder keg Garner had lit to explode. Everyone was watching Lute and Dirkson since one or the other would initiate the bloodbath.

Everyone except Fargo. He was sidling toward an outlaw on his right. He had to move as slow as molasses but if he could get his hands on a gun, Lute Garner wouldn't fight alone.

Intent on the outlaw, Fargo almost failed to register movement in the trees. He peered off into the undergrowth and discovered a pack of swarthy figures loping toward the camp like so many hungry wolves. Their faces and the bare chests of some were painted for war.

The Arapahos had caught up with those responsible for the deaths of the scouts, and they were out to extract their pound of flesh.

Fargo would just as soon the war party wiped the outlaws out. It was a fitting fate, if ever there was one.

But there were the Garners and Billy to consider. The Arapahos might plan to kill everyone and he couldn't let that happen. He needed to buy time to get Elizabeth, Mary, and Billy out of there, and there was only one way to do that. By pointing and hollering at the top of his lungs, "Indians are closing in!"

The outlaws tore their collective gazes from their leader and the gunfighter and were rooted in momentary astonishment.

"It's the stinking Arapahos!" Krist bawled.

And with that, the hounds of hell were unleashed.

Piercing war cries rose to a crescendo as the warriors bounded to the attack, only to be met by a withering hailstorm of rifle and pistol fire. Two or three dropped. The rest went to ground, and within seconds arrows began raining down.

The man guarding Fargo and Billy screeched, dropped his rifle, and tottered like a drunk. A barbed tip smeared in blood jutted from between his shoulder blades, the feathered end from his chest. He clutched at the shaft but he was already too weak to do more than give a few feeble tugs, then pitch onto his face.

The rest of the outlaws were seeking cover. No one saw Fargo scoop up the man's rifle or saw him haul Billy behind a tree and shove it into his hands. "Stay low and don't kill any Arapahos unless they're trying to kill you." Flattening, he began to crawl off but the youth grabbed his foot.

"You're leaving me alone?"

"I want what's mine," Fargo said simply, and snaked off through the weeds. The outlaws were blasting away but they were wasting lead. The Arapahos were lying low, invisible in the brush.

Someone—it sounded like Pierce—whispered loudly, "Boss! Boss! Should we make a stand or light a shuck?"

Matt Dirkson didn't answer.

Fargo carefully parted some brush. Twenty feet away a pair of grizzled forms were on their bellies behind a log. Greasy and Grimy had removed their hats and were nervously scouring the vegetation. Greasy had the Henry.

Sliding his right knee up close to his side, Fargo reached into his boot and palmed the Arkansas Toothpick. He resumed crawling.

Krist called out. "Boss? Where are you? What the hell do we do?"

Fargo dared not rise, even partway. The Arapahos might mistake him for an outlaw. Or they might be out to get him, too. He hadn't exactly parted company on the best of terms with Morning Star and Big Elk. He came within ten feet of the log. Then five.

Greasy abruptly looked over his shoulder. Instantly, Fargo pumped off the ground and sprang. Greasy spun, or tried to, in order to bring the Henry into play, but the rifle was not quite level when Fargo sheared the Toothpick into the base of Greasy's throat. Greasy jerked back and the blade popped out, and with it came a geyser of bright scarlet.

Belatedly, Grimy galvanized to life. He had a Smith and Wesson in his left hand and he swung around to fire. But Fargo clamped his free hand on Grimy's wrist. Grimy, in turn, grabbed hold of his knife hand. Locked together, they rolled back and forth, each struggling to be the first to inflict a fatal wound. In their wild thrashing, they rolled up against the log. Fargo was pinned. He tried to knee Grimy in the groin but the gunman levered onto his knees and, and with a sharp wrench, succeeded in freeing his wrist. In the blink of an eye the Smith and Wesson was pointed at Fargo's face. Fargo heard the click of the hammer.

The very next heartbeat, out of the greenery whizzed an arrow that imbedded itself in Grimy's scrawny chest. It rocked him on his knees. He gaped down at himself in dumfounded disbelief, then, gritting his teeth and hissing, he lifted his revolver to fire into the trees. Two more arrows impaled him, one in the neck, the other through his ribs. The light of life faded from his eyes and he oozed to earth like so much melted butter.

Fargo scrambled to the Henry. As he turned he saw Greasy sprawled across the log, as dead as could be.

Confusion ran rampant. The outlaws were shouting back and forth. Some wanted to make a break for it, others thought it best to stay put. Their yells pinpointed their positions, and soon arrows were finding more targets.

One voice in particular drew Fargo like a flame drew a moth. Bull Mulligan was concealed in a cluster of boulders near the meadow, and it was Mulligan who had Fargo's Colt. Crawling rapidly, Fargo circled the fire. An arrow thudded in the dirt next to his elbow. A shot from an outlaw dug a furrow under his chin.

Fargo glanced toward the tree where he had left Billy. The boy was peeking out at him, unharmed. He hoped it stayed that way.

Suddenly, from out of the boulders, rang six shots, in crisp cadence, each clipping branches and leaves a finger's-width from him. Fargo answered with the Henry, spanging rounds off the boulders, and was rewarded with a yelp of pain and a string of oaths.

Bull Mulligan burst from the boulders, one arm bleeding profusely and pressed against his side, heading for the meadow and the horses. His flight was the cue for others to flee.

Rising, Fargo dashed in among the boulders. An outlaw snapped a shot at him but missed. His own shot nearly lifted the would-be killer out of his boots.

Across the meadow two riders were galloping up the mountain. Lute and Elizabeth, the wife with their baby cradled under her shawl. Not far below them was someone else, lashing his mount with a frenzy born of stark panic. For all of Matt Dirkson's bluster, he had a yellow streak as wide as a buffalo.

Fargo took another step, intending to try to drop Dirkson, but a flurry of gunfire forced him to duck. His boot bumped something, and glancing down, he beheld his Colt, the grips red with Mulligan's blood. He wiped it clean on his pants, then twirled it into his holster. He would reload later. Right now he had to get Billy Arnold out of there.

Weaving wildly, Fargo raced toward the tree. An arrow nicked his hat, another barely missed his shoulder. Lead streaked past his ear. Both sides were doing their damnedest to kill him. But he reached the fir unscratched, and hunkering, asked, "Are you all right?"

Excitement flushed Billy's face. "Just fine! But those Indians are about to overrun us!"

Now that the outlaws were in full flight, the Arapahos were converging. Fargo saw five fleet-footed warriors approaching from different directions. Among them was Big Elk. "We're getting out of here."

An arrow thumped the trunk as Fargo turned. Another buried itself in the soil between Billy's legs. They ran for all they were worth, vaulting bodies, leaping over a log, flying pell-mell once they were clear of the trees. Outlaws were frantically trying to mount skittish horses. Others already had and were in rabid flight.

The Ovaro and the swayback were picketed at one end of the meadow along with the unshod horses. Some had broken loose and fled. Only the stallion and the swayback were in any way calm, the stallion because it was accustomed to the thunder and din of battle, the swayback because it was too old to care.

A slash of the Toothpick freed each animal. Fargo propelled Billy toward the the glue bait, snagged his saddle horn, and forked leather. A few outlaws were back-pedaling into the meadow, stragglers firing fast and furious to stem an onrushing tide of howling warriors. One outlaw shrieked and toppled, an arrow through his neck. Another took a shaft high in the shoulder. A third downed an Arapaho and was downed in turn by a precisely hurled lance.

"Fan the breeze!" Fargo shouted, and slapped the swayback on the flank. It bolted, and he matched its speed as more arrows sizzled the air. Several outlaws saw them but were too preoccupied with saving their own hides to try and stop them.

At the trail, Fargo let Billy go first so he could watch the boy's back. He shoved the Henry into the saddle scabbard to free his hands for riding as a few arrows peppered the brush. Soon they were out of range and streaking hell bent for leather for the top of the ridge.

When they were still about forty yards below the crest, Fargo spotted a knot of outlaws up above. "Rein right!" he yelled. Without hesitation, Billy obeyed, barreling through the pines like a born mountain man. They came to a clearing, and Fargo passed him and led the way from that point on, up through an aspen grove to the rim.

Several hundred yards to the west were the outlaws, waiting for the stragglers.

"What do we do now?" Billy breathlessly asked.

The answer was provided by someone else. From out of the cluster of bad men appeared Matt Dirkson. He spied them and, whipping his arm overhead, bawled, "After them, boys! A thousand dollars to whoever puts windows in their skulls!"

"Ride like the wind!" Fargo urged, and did so, racing to the northeast. They had enough of a lead that they need not worry about being shot in the back for the time being. But to hold that lead, to increase it, they had to push their horses to the limit of their endurance, and then some.

Over a mile from where the chase began was a weed-choked bench. Fargo had no sooner galloped up over the top when he spied two horses. Lute Garner was examining the front leg of one while his wife looked on in dismay. Both whirled at the pounding of the Ovaro's hooves but relaxed when they saw who it was.

"One of our animals is going lame," the gunfighter informed him. "Elizabeth and Mary will ride with me."

"You'll never make it. Dirkson and his boys aren't far behind us."

"Then I have a favor to ask, friend. See that my family and the kid make it out safely. I'll delay Dirkson long enough for all of you to get away."

"You can't delay them long enough alone. You'll need help." Fargo dismounted and gave his reins to Billy. "When your horse tires, use mine. Take Mrs. Garner straight to Fort Wise and report to the colonel."

"I'd rather stay and help you," Billy objected.

"The lady and the baby come first." Fargo drew his Colt and commenced to reload.

Lute had boosted his wife onto his horse and was handing up the baby. "Take good care of Mary. I'm relying on you to make her understand how much I loved her if worse comes to worst."

Elizabeth was trying to hold in tears and failing miserably. "We should see this through together. We're a family."

Lute lovingly touched her chin, then turned to Billy. "Get them out of here, boy! Whatever you do, don't stop, and don't look back!"

"Yes, sir." Billy was as good as his word. But Elizabeth didn't take her eyes off her husband until the forest swallowed them.

Fargo moved to the right to put some room between them. Judging by the ominous rumbling, the outlaws were almost on top of them. "How do you want to handle this?"

"Straight up."

Fargo nodded. "That suits me just fine."

From out of the pines flew Matt Dirkson, eight of his murderous crew in his wake—Mulligan, Pierce, Drecker, and Krist among them. They were moving too fast to stop in time, most with their guns already in hand. "There they are!" Dirkson screeched. "Kill the sons of bitches!"

Shots boomed like thunder.

Fargo and Lute Garner drew at the same split second

but it was Fargo's Colt that spat lead and smoke first. Two outlaws were flung from their saddles. Undaunted, the rest bore down like maddened Apaches, firing shot after shot after shot.

Fargo heard Lute grunt, then felt a stinging sensation in his left shoulder. Krist was fixing a hasty bead with a rifle to fire again. Fargo shot him in the head.

At a yell from Dirkson the outlaws fanned out. Bull Mulligan, Drecker, and another gunman made for Fargo, the rest for Lute Garner. Fargo had to make each of the four cartridges he had left in the cylinder count. He shot Drecker through the mouth, blowing out the rear of the killer's cranium in a spectacular shower of gore and brains. Pivoting so that he was standing sideways and harder to hit, he stroked the trigger again, sending a slug into the other gunman's torso. That left Bull Mulligan, fifty feet out and emptying his six-shooter like a madman. Fargo aimed carefully and nailed the cutthroat through the heart.

Lute Garner had disposed of one outlaw. Now, firing from the hip, he brought Pierce crashing down.

Matt Dirkson was the last. Miraculously unhurt, he had produced a rifle and was firing again and again. But he was no marksman.

"This is for Elizabeth and Mary," Lute declared, and fired as Dirkson fired, fired as Dirkson flung out both arms and screamed, fired as Dirkson smashed head first to the unyielding earth.

In the silence that followed Lute Garner said softly, "That felt good."

It was a week later. Skye Fargo unwrapped the Ovaro's reins from around the hitch rail in front of headquarters at Fort Wise. Across the compound, the Garners stepped from the sutler's, and waved. They were buying supplies for their trek to the Oregon country where they planned to start over. Again.

Stepping into the stirrups, Fargo had turned the stallion halfway around when a pint-sized bundle in clothes identical to his ran up. "You were going to leave without saying so long?"

"Goodbyes are for those who won't see each other again." Fargo offered his hand. "Next time I pass through, I expect to hear how well you're doing."

Billy's lower lip quivered. "I can't thank you enough for helping me land the job. I know I'll only be doing odd jobs around the post. But the colonel promised that if I apply myself, he'll let me go out with the scouts from time to time." He mustered a grin. "Before you know it, I'll be just like you."

They shook, and the boy fought back tears.

"Take care of yourself, Billy Arnold." Fargo applied his spurs harder than was his habit and trotted out the gate. He never looked back.

Mississippi River, 1861—
After the last card has been dealt
and the hand called—
Sometimes the best ace in the hole
is a loaded gun.

Skye Fargo's lake-blue eyes narrowed. After a brief moment of contemplation he threw his five poker cards on the table in front of him. "Fold," he said. A pair of deuces wasn't going to get him much.

In spite of the bad hand, Fargo thought that a steamboat casino was an inviting place to play cards. The owner of this boat, *The Wanderer,* had invested considerable money in turning what could have been a large, crude room into a well-appointed den of parquet flooring, flocked wine-colored wallpaper with matching draperies, and enough games of chance to keep two hundred gamblers busy all at the same time.

The blackjack, faro, and squirrel-cage tables took up the east section of the casino while the west was filled with various games involving dice, and four small, round tables devoted to cards. Attractive ladies employed by the casino walked among the gamblers, carrying trays of glasses filled with good whiskey and even better champagne. A gambler in his cups was an ideal gambler— he'd keep on playing even if he was losing heavily.

A man named Cameron Winthrop said, "I think Mr. Fargo is afraid to win. I think Mr. Astor here has got him scared."

There were six of them at the table. Three of them smiled. Not Fargo, nor Astor.

"If you believe those stories about me," David Astor said, "then you also believe in ghosties and goblins." He put as much sneer into his voice as he could.

"You have to admit, Astor," said Robert Daly, "it is kind of strange that four of the men who won big against you were found dead within a day's time."

"Very strange," said Kenneth Shaw.

"That damned magazine article," Astor said, sounding miserable despite the smile he'd forced his mouth to imitate.

The magazine article was the reason Skye Fargo, the Trailsman, was on the boat tonight, when he'd much rather have been somewhere else, somewhere less closed in, somewhere open to the sky.

For Men Only, a rival publication of *The Police Gazette,* had published an article about a gambler named David Astor and how, over the course of a year, every man who took home a considerable pot from one of his poker tables, four thousand dollars being the smallest of these, didn't live to see much beyond the next morning sunrise.

The magazine didn't say explicitly that Astor himself had killed the men. But the author had implied it. And while a few gamblers who practiced their craft up and down the Mississippi River generally laughed the Astor story off as a bizarre coincidence, many took it quite seriously. Even those who didn't, often kidded Astor about it without mercy.

Daly and Shaw were professional gamblers and had known Astor for years. Tonight, as most nights, they joked tirelessly about him and about each other. Sometimes there was an unpleasant edge to their humor that made Fargo wonder just how genuine their friendship for Astor really was.

Cameron Winthrop was another matter. He was a fierce, stocky man with the manner of a plantation owner. He seemed to believe that every other creature who trod the planet was his natural-born slave. In his expensive, dark Eastern-made suit, he looked the rich, spoiled man he was. He'd started chiding Astor about the article early in the evening and kept it up as midnight approached and the crowd of elegant men and women began to thin.

Because of the article, Astor had stayed away from the river for three months. Now he was gambling again, which worried his younger sister, Chloe, with whom the Trailsman had spent a blissful week once upon a time. Chloe had wired Fargo and asked him to accompany David on his trip from the Minnesota border all the way down to New Orleans.

So here he sat, playing cards and studying the men around the table. Fargo had the notion that the real killer—the person killing the players who won big against Astor—was likely somebody the young man knew. Somebody who believed he had a reason to hate David and wanted to torture him. Killing David would be too easy; he'd rather make him suffer by killing off the players who won his money. Make him such a pariah that people would be afraid to play with him. Then, maybe someday, actually get around to killing him off. If the law didn't do it first. There were four sheriffs up and down the big river who believed that Astor had killed the men, and if they could get any proof at all, Astor's days were numbered.

The man winning big tonight—the sixth man at the table—was a tipsy Colorado businessman named Fred Hollister, a novice poker player. Watching him try to cut the deck was almost embarrassing, like watching a bad vaudeville act. But the gods had blessed him this evening.

He'd already won more than thirty-five hundred dollars and he'd done so while being distracted by the bodies and charms of the roaming casino ladies. He was a grabber and a pincher and a patter, and the other men at the table were always warning him to leave the ladies alone and get back to gambling.

And for him, the gambling was going very well. It seemed that he could do no wrong. Half the time he didn't even ask for new cards, and he got so tipsy that he started knocking things over—cards, drinks, ashtrays.

Gamblers rarely brought their wives or girlfriends along on river trips. But for businessmen like Hollister and Winthrop, wives were along on every trip, and wives tended to show up to warn husbands that it was time to retire for the evening.

Mrs. Hollister was there first. A fleshy matron with an unexpectedly sweet face and manner, she stood with her hands on her husband's shoulders, only occasionally whispering for him to go. Hollister patted his wife's hands fondly when he wasn't reaching for one of the girls who drifted by. His wife tolerated his behavior with apparent good nature.

Then came Mrs. Winthrop, and the very air was charged with the kind of sexual undercurrent that quickly pulled down red-blooded men of all ages. None of the players could concentrate on their cards.

At one point, Winthrop demanded, "Will you stupid bastards quit staring at my wife and play poker?"

It was clear that the man most taken with Ida Winthrop was David Astor. He lost three hands in a row and barely seemed aware of it. From what Fargo could see, the Winthrop woman was equally taken with Astor.

And so the game went for the final forty minutes—the players greatly distracted by Ida Winthrop. Hollister was finally talked into quitting by his wife after he spilled another drink, this time all over the crotch of his tan summer suit.

Cam Winthrop was drunk, too, but where Hollister was a happy drunk, Winthrop was angry and suspicious of everything.

"No you don't," he snapped at Fargo when the Trailsman cut the deck for one more hand. "You waited 'til I was distracted to cut them. Now cut them again in front of me."

Fargo shrugged. It wasn't worth arguing about, not with a drunk. He cut the cards again.

But Winthrop's main opponent was not Fargo; David Astor took that role. For the last six hands, Winthrop had maneuvered the game so that he and Astor were the only two still tossing money into the pot. The last game Winthrop obviously felt he'd won—a trio of jacks, queen high. But then he saw the cards Astor laid on the table.

A trio of queens, a pair of threes.

"You're trash!" Winthrop shouted imperiously. "Every goddamned one of you! River trash! Gutter trash!"

By now, most of the people in the casino were aware that a scene was playing out. In casinos, scenes happened with the regularity of busted flushes. Casino regulars were used to raised voices, shoving matches, bellowed threats. They'd pay each a minute or two of attention, then go back to their games.

Winthrop grabbed his wife and tore her away from the casino. But not before she got one last lingering look at David Astor.

Astor was still staring at the space the beautiful blond angel had just inhabited when Shaw laughed. "I'd let that one go, David."

"Did you see her?" Astor said.

"We saw her," Shaw said.

"And we also saw him," Daly said.

"He's the kind of self-important son of a bitch who could buy his way out of murdering somebody, Davey," Shaw said.

"I'm going to see to it that you get to your room right away tonight," Fargo said to Astor.

"My nursemaid," Astor said bitterly. "Thank you, sis-ter Chloe."

"Your sister did you a favor, kid," Shaw said. "Fargo here's gonna make sure you live to see New Orleans."

"Yeah, and I'll be a virgin when I get there," Astor said.

Shaw yawned. "Right. Well, I'm going to turn in. Now that Mrs. Winthrop is gone, I just don't feel like sitting here and looking at you ugly bastards."

Daly said, "Look who's talking about being ugly. You couldn't get laid with a Winchester and a bag of gold."

Fargo laughed. He could never quite be sure if those two disliked each other as much as their bantering indi-cated. One thing for sure, they definitely enjoyed ragging on each other.

"Turning in doesn't sound like a bad idea," Astor said. He yawned, too.

Fargo studied Astor a long suspicious moment. The twenty-two-year-old never went to bed this early.

Astor was the first to stand. He stretched and yawned again. Both times seemed a little theatrical to Fargo. What was the kid planning, anyway? If he hadn't liked Astor's sister so much, Fargo would've gladly walked away. Being a nursemaid wasn't his style, and neither was floating down rivers on steamboats. The kid was old enough to fend for himself. Even when people accused him of murder.

"You ready to go, nurse?" Astor asked Fargo.

Daly and Shaw grinned. Daly said, "Makes a nice story for a magazine. 'Skye Fargo Was My Nursemaid.' "

"More like 'Skye Fargo Was My Jailer,' " Astor said. There was an acrimonious tone in his voice.

"I don't like it any more than you do, kid," Fargo said. "But that sister of yours can be damned persuasive when she wants to be."

A slender blond serving girl stopped by the table and began picking up the empty glasses. Her breasts gave her peasant blouse a most pleasing fullness while her colorful skirt lent her hips a provocative richness.

As she leaned over Fargo's shoulder for his glass, she said, "Do you have a lucky number?"

Clever, too, Fargo thought. In addition to being pretty. "Well, my cabin number's twenty-three. Maybe that'll bring me some luck tonight."

"Twenty-three," she repeated. "Yes, that could bring you some very good luck tonight."

And then she was gone.

Shaw, standing up, doing some stretching of his own, said, "You and that girl couldn't have been more obvious if you tried."

"Jealousy," Fargo said with a laugh. "Pure jealousy. Three gamblers who'll be sleeping alone tonight just can't stand the idea of anyone else indulging in some tasty female wine while they scratch and fart in their sleep."

They all left the casino in good moods.

The night was cool, the moon full. They'd gone into the casino around five o'clock. The vessel had still been moving down the vast river. It would keep moving during the night because the bright moonlight on the mile-wide tide would be enough for the pilot to steer by.

The men went on their way, and Fargo wondered again who was out to get Astor. There are people who hate anybody else's success. It becomes a sickness with them, their hatred; they spend much of their time nurturing the envy, the hatred. And then a small percentage act on it. In the case of Astor, his persecutor had figured out a unique way of getting to the young man. Make it look as if Astor was killing any opponent who beat him. Keep it up, and Astor wouldn't be able to buy his way into a game with a sack of gold as big as the boat they were on.

Astor yawned and said, "Nice night."

"Better out here," Fargo said. "I don't know how you fellas can sit in there so long. All the smoke and the noise and the card games. A couple of hours of that would last me for a couple of months. But you're in there day and night."

"Wait'll we get to New Orleans and that big poker game. It'll be a lot worse."

"Your sister's going to be damned mad if I'm not there with you," Fargo said.

"You're probably right about that, but I don't much like being watched over."

"Get some sleep, David. I'll see you in the morning."

Astor said, "I'll bet that serving girl's already in your cabin waiting for you."

"Well, she did say that twenty-three was my lucky number."

Fargo hurried to his cabin, to see if the number would indeed bring him luck tonight.

No other series has this much historical action!

THE TRAILSMAN

To order call: 1-800-788-6262

JASON MANNING

S575